# AN OLD PUB NEAR THE ANGEL

Also by James Kelman in Polygon

*The Busconductor Hines*
*A Chancer*
*Not not while the giro*

# AN OLD PUB NEAR THE ANGEL

## THE ANGEL

### And Other Stories

## James Kelman

First published in 1973 by Puckerbrush Press, USA.
This edition published in 2007 by Polygon,
an imprint of Birlinn Ltd

West Newington House
10 Newington Road
Edinburgh
EH9 1QS

www.birlinn.co.uk

9 8 7 6 5 4 3 2 1

The publisher acknowledges subsidy from the

Scottish
**Arts** Council
**LOTTERY FUNDED**

towards the publication of this volume.

ISBN 10: 1 84697 037 7
ISBN 13: 978 1 84697 037 5

*British Library Cataloguing-in-Publication Data*
A catalogue record for this book is available on request from the British Library.

Typeset in Minion by Palimpsest Book Production Limited,
Grangemouth, Stirlingshire
Printed and bound by
Clays Ltd, St Ives plc

# Contents

# The Cards

'Duncan your record is appalling,' Sanderson looked over his head somewhere and then sniffed. 'You should have been fired the last time you were up.'

'But Mr Sanderson there were reasons for those absences,' Duncan stopped and looked away.

'What excuses could there be for this,' he picked up the folder, 'since the last time you were up here. Look at this.' He smacked the page with his left hand. 'November sixth, eight, nine, the fourteenth, twentieth, twenty-first and twenty-second.' Sanderson let the page fall.

'But I gave a medical certificate for those three days,' said Duncan.

'No that won't do,' Sanderson frowned. 'I mean what would my bosses think. No. You'll be paid to the end of the week. Now let me see, Tuesday isn't it.'

'Yes.'

'Fine fine,' he made a note on a pad then sat back in his modern chair.

'Well Duncan if you go home and change now, you could get to the stores before it closed. Or you could go tomorrow. Yes perhaps that would be best.'

'I won't be working today then?'

'Today!' His eyebrows arched in astonishment. 'No, no,' Sanderson sucked in air sharply between clenched teeth making a rasping sound. 'No!' he said again loudly and shook his balding head violently.

Duncan stood up. 'The cards be ready tomorrow as well?'

Sanderson stared curiously up at Duncan, taking in the semi-long hair and then, lowering his gaze, noticing the crew neck sweater under the uniform jacket, said: 'I don't think you were suited for this type of job from the start you know.'

Duncan felt the blood roaring through his head. Christ what an insult. It really was.

'Try and collect your things before 2.30 eh?' murmured Sanderson picking up the telephone receiver.

He wondered whether Sanderson could hear his heart thumping.

The anger subsided. 'OK, Mr Sanderson I'll see you.' He turned and opened the door. Sanderson began dialling a number. His secretary looked up at Duncan as he walked across to the front door.

Duncan paused and smiled. 'Little shite isn't he?'

The woman turned in her swing chair and pulled out a drawer from the filing cabinet.

He closed the door behind him and walked out the gate to the bus stop. Well that was that. It was good to be free again. Still December? Bad time of the year for the broo. Probably be barred for misconduct. Yes bad timekeeping Mr Duncan ah ha. The ultimate sin, matched only by raping the district superintendent's wife. Still the NAB would have to pay. A wife and child?

'Jake Duncan!' called out a youth in a bus conductor's uniform.

Duncan looked round. 'Aye Alec how's it goin'?'

'Not bad.' The conductor pointed to the office. 'What were you in for?'

'Absences, late reports,' Duncan shrugged, 'the bullet.'

'Jesus Christ! Must have been pretty bad for that.'

'Aye,' he looked up the road.

'Could do wi' a holiday myself,' said Alec smiling.

'Aye,' replied Duncan. 'Anyway looks like my bus coming.'

'Yeah sure Jake,' he grinned, 'might see you in Bells sometime.'

'Probably. Oh Alec any fags?'

'Aye.' Alec produced a ten packet. 'Want a couple?'

'Aye if you can spare them man.'

'What with the fiddle I've got, are you kidding?' Alec gave him three.

Jake burst out laughing and shook his head. 'What a fucking job.'

The bus drew in to the kerb and Duncan stepped on to the platform. He turned and said, 'See you Alec,' then walked upstairs, to sit in the back seat. He caught a last glimpse of the garage before the bus turned the sharp bend into the main Glasgow road.

Duncan knew every bump and hill on this road, he could also name every pub and betting shop between Garthill and the boundary. He settled back and closed his eyes. He had always found it easy to sleep on a bus, too easy at times.

Not a bad job the buses. Hours were terrible right enough but you could knock up a decent wage if you put in the hours. Christ it was a bad time of the year for the broo. She'd be worried. Understatement. Probably go off her head. Could take a couple of part-time jobs. Mark a board or a boozer. Done them before. Anyway, time for a pint before going home. She's not expecting me back till midnight anyway. Could stay out for a while. Maybe win a few quid on the horses. Who knows?

The journey to Killermont Street from Garthill Bus Depot took forty-five minutes exactly and when Jake alighted, it was 2.30 p.m., just too late for a pint. He had 4/- in his pocket and all the time in the world to spend it. Not enough for the Pictures but he could have a bet or a table game at snooker. No fags though.

Jake walked over to the kiosk and bought a half ounce of Sun Valley and a packet of Rizlas. He would have to rely on travelling free on the bus. The Corporation and other omnibus companies' employees had an unofficial agreement whereby drivers and conductors were never asked for fares while travelling in uniform. Occasionally Jake had had to pay on a Corporation bus because the conductor had been an old timer and old timers were notorious company men. They had worked on the trams and boy it was a job in those days – had to wear white collar, black tie and black shoes then. Better than the average wages too. Aye, aye. Aye! NOT like now. Not at all.

He decided to go home and tell Joan. Better to get it over and done with. He walked down Buchanan Street pausing at Gerrards corner. The Man's Shop, there was a good tie in the window he rather fancied. Perhaps get it for Christmas. Buchanan Street was crowded with Christmas shoppers especially at Argyle Street and where the expensive stores were. A tie could cost five and a half quid there. Argyle Street was busier yet with thousands of people charging around clutching paper bags and shopping bags. When the traffic lights changed they surged across the road and the red-necked traffic policeman was powerless to do anything other than wave them on. Less than two weeks to go and the urge was upon the people to buy and buy and buy in time for Xmas.

The bus queue outside Arnott's stretched for thirty yards and Jake joined the end. Unfortunately he had to queue like anyone else because he worked on the blue buses and therefore had no priority.

The people waiting were complaining and Jake listened amused. Apparently there had not been a 63 or 64 through for nearly twenty minutes and it was beginning to snow. A wee man standing next to Jake opened the left corner of his mouth.

'Bloody freezing isn't it?'

'Aye' replied Jake.

'Bloody snow,' the wee man spat into the gutter, turned his coat collar up and pulled his bunnet down tighter until it rested on his ears.

'What is that son?' he pointed to a bus standing at the traffic lights. 'Is that a 64?' he asked.

'No it's a 63,' said Jake.

'Jesus Christ!' The wee man hunched his shoulders up and turned inwards. The lights changed to green and the bus drew into the stop; three people got down and the conductress leaned out. 'First three,' she called.

About eight women jumped on defiantly.

'I said the first three!'

'We've been waiting half an hour you know,' said one woman.

'What a shame,' replied the conductress, 'wait and I'll get the ladders out and you can climb on the roof.'

'There's no' even five standing,' said another but the automatic doors closed on the reply. The bus pulled away but stopped again and the doors opened.

'Hey Jake!' shouted the driver.

Duncan recognized him and jumped on unaware of the accusing looks from the people left behind.

'Harry,' he said, 'when did you start in here?'

'Three months ago,' replied the driver as he closed the doors and drove off. 'Better than that mob you're with.'

'Wouldn't be hard,' said Jake. 'I jacked today anyway.'

'Yeah?'

'Well they asked me to leave.'

'So long as you got your refs,' said the driver.

'Oh I made sure of that.' They both laughed.

'Why don't you start in here man?'

'No Harry. I'm finished with the buses. For the time being anyway,' said Jake.

The bus was passing under Central Bridge and the driver asked, 'Anybody wanting off?'

'No,' said Jake looking down the passage.

'Hang on then,' Harry said. The people queuing at the bus stop had their hands out expectantly, the driver slowed the bus down a little, drawing in to the kerb, then he accelerated and waved goodbye as he drove off across Hope Street.

Jake burst out laughing. 'What a fucking job.'

'Listen to the punters,' said Harry grinning. They were all talking excitedly across to each other and pointing to the driver's cabin at the front. The conductress came downstairs smiling. She was around thirty and smartly dressed.

'You've got them all going now,' she said, 'listen to that babble.'

'Did you see the look on the faces at the bus stop?' asked Jake.

'Serve them right,' she said, and walked down to collect the fares. The chatter stopped dramatically.

'They know Sheila too well,' said Harry. 'When she starts they know all about it.'

'Aye I could believe that,' smiled Jake.

'Oh she's OK. Been in the job about ten years,' said Harry. The conductress returned and passed round the cigarettes.

'Where you living Jake?' asked Harry after a time.

'In Partick man, Beith Street.'

'That's next to the garage.'

'Aye just before Sandy Road.'

The bus pulled into the lights at Partick Cross.

'Room and kitchen, inside toilet,' Jake continued.

'Bought?' asked Sheila.

'No. Six quid a month including rates. They're coming down though.'

'Aye you'll get a corporation house,' said Sheila.

'That's very nice, probably get a semi-detached out Castlemilk,' said the driver.

'Aye,' Jake smiled wryly, 'or the Drum.'

'My sister lives in Drumchapel,' said Sheila, 'and she quite likes it. Depends what part you get I suppose.'

'Aye,' replied Jake, 'anyway this is where I get off.'

'Aye. Listen Jake take a run up to the Wheatsheaf one night. I'm early all week. Definitely be in on Friday night.'

'Yeah I'll probably do that,' he stepped down. 'See you later.'

He walked down Crawford Street which was nearly all down now. Only the top and bottom closes remained and the old detached house near the railway line was boarded up.

Jake was beginning to feel very depressed at the thought of explaining it all to Joanie. He turned in to No. 136 and trod on an old shit.

'Bastard!' he grunted without anger, and wiped his shoe with a piece of newspaper. The headline caught his eye. He read aloud. '"Baxter to leave Rangers?" Christ what is it all about.' He looked at the date and snorted, '1966.'

He walked upstairs. The steps were cracked and chipped, condensation seeped from the scarlet painted walls. Gang slogans and names and dates were scrawled everywhere in paint of all colours. The Duncans lived on the top floor across the landing from the Moonans. He knocked at the door and heard his wife come through from the kitchen. He could see a shadow in the peephole he had put in the door. It opened a slit then widened.

'Jackie?' said the girl in surprise.

'Hullo,' he entered and kissed her. 'Well where's the milkman then?'

She smiled at the old joke. 'Are you on a spread over?'

'No, eh,' he grimaced, 'they fired me, any tea?' he went through to the kitchen and filled the kettle. He plugged it in.

'Jackie what is it?' She stood by the door. 'Jackie what's happened?'

'I got the sack,' he shrugged, 'bad timekeeping.'

7

'Oh.'

'Could do with a couple of weeks' holiday anyway.'

Joan sat down heavily in her armchair.

'I'll have three weeks' wages coming to me,' said Jake coming to her.

'Oh Jackie,' said the girl. 'What . . .'

'Listen I can get a job right away if you want?' he interrupted.

She looked up at him, 'Where?'

'The Corporation for goodness sake,' he put his hand on her shoulder, 'no bother.'

She got up as the kettle boiled. 'Tea?'

'Aye. I thought I'd wait till after the New Year before starting.'

'Some New Year,' she poured the water into the teapot.

'Och come on for God's sake,' said Jake quietly.

'What happens if they don't take you?' she asked.

'They're crying out for men,' replied Jake, 'anyway I might take on a couple of wee side jobs.'

She sighed. 'Like what?'

'Marking a board. Maybe a boozer, oh there's plenty going about.'

He accepted a cup from her and sipped slowly.

'Then I'll never see you,' she sighed again sadly, 'I hardly see you as it is.'

'At least I won't be working shifts.'

'Can you get a job as a salesman?' she asked.

'Need a couple of suits.'

'You've got two.'

'Och they're hopeless,' Jake answered, 'I never wear them as it is.' He rolled a cigarette.

'Thought you had stopped smoking?'

'I'm finished buying packets,' he gave a short laugh, 'only 3/8 for a half ounce.'

He stood up and undressed. 'Do you know where my trousers are?'

'The blue ones?' replied Joanie.

'Aye.'

'In the wardrobe, unless you've shifted them.'

He went through to the room and found them hanging in the wardrobe. The baby was gurgling away to herself. He leaned over the cot and made her laugh.

His wife came through just as he picked the baby up.

'Is she wet?' asked she.

'Aye and smelly,' grinned Jake dancing around with the baby.

'I met Mum this morning,' she said. 'Asked when we were coming round.'

'What did you say?' he asked.

'Said I'd phone.'

'We'll go round tomorrow night.'

'Dad could get you in beside him,' she said cautiously.

'Is that so,' replied Jake showing no interest.

'He's offered before Jackie.'

'Yeah I know,' he handed the baby to her, 'yes I might.'

'Will I say anything?'

'NO!' He spoke sharply. 'No leave it for a while yet.'

'OK,' the girl said it quietly. 'What do you want for tea?'

'Stew made the same as you did it last Friday.'

'OK,' she smiled and walked from the room carrying the baby.

Jake picked out a book and sat down to read.

# A Roll for Joe

It was a modern pub, quite a flash sort of place. Piped music and the obligatory slot machine. Tables along the wall and high stools at the bar. A brewery house but not too bad.

'Pint of bitter please.'

Quite a pleasant grunt from this skinny bartender.

'Not a bad night eh?'

'Yeah,' he jerked it out the corner of thin lips.

'Spring. Good season eh?'

He shrugged and plonked the pink glass down on the mosaic counter. Some froth sloshed over the rim and streamed towards my elbow.

'Two and five.'

I got my penny change and sat on a high stool. Hell of a job being a barman. Watching everybody bevying the night away man. Must be pretty bad. All the conversations. Having to talk or at least acknowledge all the pieces of chat. No wonder you look so bored Percy. Why don't you rob the till and high tail it to the badlands. That beer was very good.

'Hey give us another pint man will you?' Not even rinsing the glass out. Percy. Percy. You'll never make the big time going to those games.

'Hullo Joe how you going,' said the barman to a newcomer. A man in his forties, average build although a bit overweight.

'Brown and mild Freddie. When you're ready.' The fellow looked around nodding to one or two patrons. Oh to be an accepted regular. Oh God the glory.

'Two and five.'

'Anything to eat?'

'Not a bad night Joe.'

'Yeah.' Joe nodded.

'Nuts and crisps.'

'Finished are you?' The snidey bartender paid no attention as he made up a brown and mild.

'All finished Freddie. Yes finished for the day.'

'Want any?'

'Any what?'

'Nuts and crisps.'

'Oh!' Up you Freddie. 'No!'

'Two and five,' he pushed the brown and mild gently across to the regular.

'Give us a whisky as well.' The barman turned to a bottle of brewery Joe Bloggs whisky.

'Any good ones?'

'Good ones?'

Now Percy why do you look at Joe! Is there something lacking? Are you inferior? What is this moral support business?

'Like what?'

'Give us a glass of that. That black label man. Next to the Emva cream.'

He counted each drip into the tumbler smiling to himself.

'Eight and eleven.'

I paid up and lit a cigarette. Perhaps I could join their talk.

'How's the missus?' asked the worker.

'Pooo.'

'Like that. Yeah,' Freddie nodded knowing it all.

'Aye, aye,' I muttered from the boots.

Both looked at me.

'Aye, this married business,' I shook my head in summing up.

11

'Yeah. You're right Jock,' agreed Joe. 'Married yourself?'

'Once upon a time.'

That's a downright lie gents.

'Has its good points Joe.' Freddie nodded to emphasise, 'Must admit that.'

'Pooo!'

'Aye.'

'On your own now are you?' asked Joe as Freddie went to another customer.

'Yeah,' I winked, 'the only way to be man.'

'Lucky bastard.' Poor old Joe lit up a cigarette. 'Yeah.' He muttered, exhaling a little smoke, 'Yeah.'

'Kids?'

'Two of them Jock. Yeah two of them.'

What else is there to say. That's nice? What is there?

'And . . .' I began.

'Trouble? Pooo nothing but bleedin trouble Jock.'

'Yeah?'

'Yeah. Once a kid reaches fourteen! Look out.' Joe glanced around the room and thrust one hand deep into his trouser pocket. His shoulders hunched as he shook his head.

'Why I come in here, init?'

'Yeah?'

'Why else? Place like this. Pathetic.'

'What'll you have Joe?'

He looked, trying to figure it out.

'Eh.'

'C'mon.'

'I'll have a gin and a bottle of brown then Jock cheers.'

'Hey give us a gin, another black label and bottle of brown and a bottle of light ale.'

The barman looked at Joe and then back to me once more.

'Have one yourself man.'

'I'll have a brown mate thanks.'

'He's OK,' said Joe.

'Drink in here regularly then?'

'Most evenings at opening times. Sometimes stay on till late.'

'Here lads,' the barman downed half his beer, his nose wrinkling as he put the glass back on the counter.

'Not very busy is it?'

'Not at nights Jock. No. Lunch hour trade mostly,' he nodded his head. 'Busy then. That right Joe? Live around here do you?' after a pause.

'Quite near.'

'Drink up Jock.'

'What?' I swallowed the whisky.

'Drink up.' Joe stood counting out some money. 'Same again Freddie. No beer though. Not for me. Had a drink earlier.'

'Nor me man, whisky's plenty.' I drank some light ale to clear my mouth. 'Want a plain Joe?'

'No I'll stick to the tipped.'

We lit up and remained silent until the round of drinks arrived.

'What do you do Joe? For a living I mean.'

'Piss-ball about in a printing shop, that's what I do.'

I laughed, 'Jesus.'

Joe grinned, 'Why what do you do?'

'Nothing man, I don't really do anything.'

'Are you a drop out?'

'I don't think so Joe, never been in anywhere to drop out. No I just don't work. Had a job a couple of years ago right enough. Desperate at the time.'

'Well, good luck if you can get away with it. Cheers.' He finished the gin but I let the whisky remain where it was.

'Freddie another gin and light ale.' I turned to Joe and said, 'I've got to be going soon.'

'You're a bit well dressed to be a drop out,' mused Joe.

'What age are your kids?'

'One's twenty-two now, the girl's eighteen,' he grunted to himself.

'What do they do?'

'God knows. Don't even know where he is.' He looked at me. 'He's a bloody drop out I think. One of the neighbours thinks she saw him up west a couple of weeks ago. Hair down to his ankles she said. Fits the description anyway. His mother wants me to look for him.' Joe laughed bitterly. 'Where would I look for him?'

'I don't know, there's places you could look for him.'

'Would you look for him?'

'I wouldn't.'

'Course you're the same as him. Are you in advertising?'

'Jesus. Not me Joe.'

He shook his head trying to suss it all out. 'No, can't reckon you at all. You a pop singer for God's sake.'

'Think I'd be in here bevying?'

'Of course, of course. Scotch? Footballer that's what you are. Think you're Georgie Best. Yeah.'

'Wrong again.'

'What's wrong with all you bastards Jock. Just can't understand it any.' He went silent and noticing the barman hanging about, called the same again.

'Listen I went through the war and detested nearly every minute of it. All those bastard officers. Walking over the top of us and poncing around shouting orders at you. Christ it was bad. I never bore anybody with details about it like some do. I mean I . . .' Freddie was standing waiting for payment.

'Listen Jock,' Joe collected the change, 'listen Jock here's us having a drink together, I'm forty-nine and what are you? Twenty-four or something?' I nodded.

'I mean we're quite enjoying the chat aren't we? But we could come to blows any minute. Let's face it.'

'I know what you mean Joe.'

'You don't know what I mean son.'

I nodded slowly. 'I know exactly what you mean.'

He snapped his fingers. 'A student.'

'No not me Joe.'

'You know exactly what I mean,' his eyes twinkling out with something deeper, he poked his forefinger into my chest. 'Tell me what I'm talking about son.'

'The age gap. Generation gap that's all.' I sat back nearly falling from the stool.

'Look at you just now son. Just about fell off the bloody stool there. What's wrong? Can't you hold your drink?'

I smiled contemptuously, 'What does it matter.'

'Shouldn't drink if you can't stomach it son.' He laughed, 'that's the trouble with you bastards, think you're men cause you're old enough to go into a pub.'

'Listen man I'm twenty-five and divorced. Don't talk to me like your wee boy or something.'

'Listen man. Man, Man, Man. Why do you say man all the time.'

'Same reason you say son I suppose.'

'Don't give me that Jock. Freddie!'

The barman walked over.

'Same again and one for yourself.'

'It's my round man.'

Joe pulled a face. 'I'm buying.'

'It's my turn.'

'What you talking about. Turn. I'm buying, OK!'

'What's wrong Joe, does it make you feel good to do all the buying or something. Superior, do you feel superior is this it?'

'Pooo.'

I shook my head. When Freddie returned with the drinks I immediately ordered the same again with beer as chasers.

Joe smiled, not wholly sarcastic.

'You're all right Jock. Drunk but all right.'

Christ this fellow was getting on my nerves.

'Who's bloody drunk man.' I drank half of the whisky to prove it.

'D'you like the printing game?' I asked blinking as the drink hit my toes.

'Money for old rope.'

'Are you a printer?' Christ my stomach.

'No labourer.'

'Machine minder?'

'Yeah. Ah it's not bad. Good money. Strong union.'

The whisky was becoming harder to get down. I stepped down from the stool very deliberate in my movements.

'Second on the left,' said Joe pointing to a door. I nodded and set off. Christ it was difficult to negotiate a clear round. Have to calm down with the drink man. Don't let him needle me into getting pished. I pushed the lavatory door open. One old timer stood peeing, one hand supporting him against the wall. A scratched black pipe clenched between his gums, he mumbled something about old Enoch being a boy all right, then he farted and sniggered. 'Bloody mice,' he said. I finished and splashed the cold water on my face and neck. Much better. Much better indeed. I left the old guy to his toil and marched back to my seat.

'Thought you'd gone home then.'

'Who me?' I pointed to my chest, 'With all that yellow peril hanging about. Jesting?'

I tilted back the glass, 'Cheers Joe,' I finished it.

'Been in London long?'

'On off about five years.'

'That long eh?'

'Yeah. Always come back here eventually.'

'Born here myself.'

'Oh.'

'Yeah down Kentish Town way.'

'Where d'you live now?'

'Got a house out Wood Green.'

'Quite nice out there.'

Joe wrinkled his face. 'Yeah got a garden and that.'

'Neighbours all right?'

He stared at me for about a minute curiously then said, 'I know you Jock,' nodding his head with certainty. I sipped the light ale and lit a cigarette before replying.

'I don't know you Joe.'

'What do you do again?'

'Nothing man. I don't do anything.'

Joe sighed and began tapping his fingers on the glass.

'You're a strange bastard.'

'Not me Joe.' I glanced at the clock above the gantry. Nearly an hour and a half till closing.

'Yeah Jock you.' Joe put his glass down firmly on the counter and stepped back swaying a little.

'I'm off for a piss.'

'I'll get another round up.' I smiled but Joe did not return it.

A man sitting alone near the door gazed up questioningly but I slowly shook my head. He looked away. Ten minutes passed before Joe returned. He had obviously gone through the cold water routine and appeared steadier on his feet now.

'Ah Jock,' he said heavily, 'some life eh?'

'I doubt if I'll get this whisky down.'

'Never try the gin then?'

'Bloody perfume man.'

'Oh it's good. Pleasant to the taste.'

'What does your girl do?'

'Hairdressing. At college. Yeah.' Joe smiled to himself. 'Ah she's quite a girl Jock. Yeah.'

We remained silent for two minutes. I was finding some difficulty in concentrating. Joe appeared to be quite fresh which rather surprised me. He looked at his watch.

'Time I hit the road,' he lit another cigarette.

'Already?'

'Christ you were talking about leaving two hours ago.'

'Aye, but I was enjoying the chat.'

'Pooo.'

'I was Joe.'

'Anyway.' He glanced quickly around the room. 'I'll see you again son.'

I gave him a sort of salute and smiled. 'Cheerio man.' Joe turned and marched across the floor and out. The man at the door rose slowly, nodded over to me and followed him out.

Poor old Joe.

# Abject Misery

He was in his third month of poverty-stricken freedom and
fast losing most of his friends including the one commonly
known as his best. It couldn't last much longer. He checked
his pockets, again discovering that 1½d. which had haunted
him since Monday night. He also had the usual fruitless search
for forgotten fags and butt ends. He couldn't understand how
he'd managed to survive the past three days. One of these
days he'd have to get a job. This no money was becoming a
problem. How was one supposed to eat? He spoke aloud,
'God, how is one supposed to eat? I mean fair do's and all
that piss.' Lapsing into a depressed silence he lay staring at
the ceiling until remembering about the hotel up west. The
one that served meals to all their employees and all the people
who worked in other hotels in the chain. No questions or
raised eyebrows he'd heard. Why not take the chance. Of
course it would mean having to leave this lovely, warm and
tender, dirty, scratchy kip. Still it was worth it. He got out of
bed. It was so cold. Why do landlords never supply electric
fires? Only those shitey gas fires needing shitey tanners. This
was really terrible. Why not huge roaring logs burning and
hot toddies. Danish blue cheese and french bread. Twenty
Players and a bird. Oh man. They definitely do not care about
their lodgers in this place. You could starve or freeze to death.
Have to do a moonlight, that would show the bastard, course
old John would probably hang out the flags. Christ imagine
having a right few quid though. Maybe get a real good place

with fitted carpets, refrigerators and TV sets. Easy to get a chick up then with a bit of comfort around.

He lifted a towel and walked over to the sink.

No on reflection why wash? The water would be ice cold. Could possibly die of heart failure when it splashed the face. Why take the chance? Nobody would know the difference anyway.

He walked back and quickly dressed.

Have to get down to the laundrette shortly, the socks are beginning to crack. It must be great to be able to put on a fresh pair of pants and maybe a vest. Still, at least I can dress quite respectably on the outside. Thank God I can't find a pawn shop that accepts clothes. Hope I don't get knocked back at this hotel canteen, Christ that would just about finish me. Oh just imagine though, chicken fricassaise or something. No. No. Curried chicken with all the etceteras oh man man cups of tea, one during and two after. Perhaps someone will offer a polite fag afterwards who knows.

He had a look in the mirror screwing up his face and smoothing his untidy hair into order with both hands then he turned and left the room. As he locked the door one of the other tenants happened to be climbing the stairs carrying a brush and shovel.

'Well Charles,' he said, 'got a start yet?'

'Why, no Mr Reilly. Have not got a start yet.'

'Why don't you try building sites. Always plenty of work going there eh?' he smiled.

'Yeah that's a good idea, thanks. Might just do that.'

'Yes it would get you back on your feet again eh?'

'That's right, it would put me back on my feet again. Ha ha.'

'Well, anyway,' he smiled uneasily, 'got some cleaning to do eh? Ha ha. No rest for the wicked eh?'

'That's right ha ha.' Yeah hurry away you miserable, 'Oh Mr

Reilly,' he turned, 'Mr Reilly could you spare a fag, haven't had a chance to . . . thanks, ta . . . bye.'

Charles walked downstairs, paused, scanning the piles of mail and left without checking to see if he had any.

At least it had stopped raining. Also Charles had cheered up. He enjoyed walking, normally he had no choice, money was too scarce to waste on bus or tube fares. God please let me find two and six lying on the pavement. Hey look at the bent-looking idiot – wonder if that's the only nose he has. His gait man look at his gait. Take one look at me you bastard and you will need a new nose. Oh quite a nice looking chick over there. Hullo there she's looking across. Wink at her, no response. Yeah thanks for returning it, nice of you to acknowledge it with a quirk of the lips or friendly smile. Actually you are a hackit-looking bag, so there. Ha Ha Ha. Jasus another, look at the walk on her, definitely the girl from Ipanema.

'Good morning Astrud,' he called. The girl looked startled and hurried away. Ah well at least you noticed me. The crack was a bit above your level anyhow. Sorry darling but there it is. Not your fault. Man. Oh. Thought that was a tanner there – might have saved the old legs a couple of miles' slog. Or perhaps a couple of scones from that dairy. Ah never mind. Still though imagine having lived on Britain's green and pleasant land for twenty-three years and not a tosser to show for it, apart from the faithful 1½d. Look at John Stevens too, a bloody millionaire at twenty-six. Christ look at The Beatles. No man, I'll definitely have to change my ways. I mean it this time. Get a job and a good flat. Really go to town – do it all up – get a cocktail cabinet, that's a must – have a few bottles of Dimple and Drambuie – all the best gear. Brandy of course – vodka too and Bacardi for the women. One of those boxes containing at least a hundred fags. The fridge of course, cheese and steak and ice cubes, crates of Guinness and lager. Christ imagine it, ninety-six mohair suits and thirty-four Crombie coats and . . .

He stepped off the kerb, right into a deep puddle.

'For FUCK's sake,' he shouted, and stepped back again noticing the startled expressions of the shocked passers-by.

God love us, step into a bloody puddle, dirty filthy water and dogs' pish gets over the tops of your shoes soaking your socks and feet and you can't even shout fuck. Ach I'm really sick of it all. Must get a job, this would never have happened if I could of afforded a bus. What a life. Oh man man this is really bad. I'll be squelching and sliding in my shoes all day now. Wonder how far it is to Blackfriars?

'Excuse me passer-by, how far is . . .' The girl walked on hurriedly. Jesus you'd think I was going to rape her or something. What a look, an honest simple question. Wish I knew what was with some people. Wonder how long it takes to cross this road. Man, look at this face. God love us. Imagine having one like that. Course he'll have money though – that's the difference. I'd take his face in a minute, if his money went with it. Ah the poor old bastard, probably got a heavy mortgage – overdrawn at the bank – wife pregnant for the seventeenth time and every one a mongol.

'I'm sorry mister,' he shouted aloud, the man, hearing the call, turned back.

'What?' asked the man.

'Harry. I'm Harry, oh sorry I thought you were Mr Jackson.'

'What?' asked the man, evidently wondering what it was all about.

'OK? Sorry about that.' Charles began edging away, the man was still standing.

Ah well that'll teach me. Should of asked him for a light there. But – this nice-looking chick will do fine.

'Excuse . . .' too late, the girl was halfway down the road.

Charming. You'd think my fly was open with the business

hanging out, I mean man, just running away like that it's enough to make me go bent or something. Oh quick.

'Hey mister, have you a light please?'

'Yes son.'

'Thanks a lot. Thanks. Ta. Thanks an awful.'

'That's OK son.'

So grateful I nearly kissed him there.

Charles inhaled deeply and immediately burst into a fit of uncontrollable coughing, causing looks of concern from one or two onlookers. He spat. The catarrh was so green and thick it bounced off the ground.

'My goodness!' cried the gathering crowd in unison.

Jesus Christ this is disgusting, I'll have to see a doctor. Imagine dying of cancer at twenty-three it would make you sick. Old Grandpa died of cancer. Course he had a good long life, no complaints there. But twenty-three? Malnutrition probably has something to do with it. Hey look at her man, what a coupon, legs like a billiard table. I bet even she'd knock me back.

Have to pack this existence in. Start looking for a job tomorrow after I get paid, may even do a moonlight tomorrow night. Hope I don't see John though, course the old bastard knows I see the NAB man on Thursdays. Ah shite, who cares. Charles noticed an amusement arcade not far from Blackfriars Bridge, he flipped a coin and entered. Ah the dog machine, wonder what to back. Hey how come I'm the only punter in here, must be crooked or something. Never mind I'll try the red dog – only evens of course but still, if I can do a three timer I'll have a tanner then try the slots and the sky's the limit. Right. They're off Park Royal running 3.36, it's six from two, three, one and four. On the one dog. Round the bottom bend it's three going on from two, four one – round the final bend it's three going two lengths clear of two. On the one dog. Go on my son. Ah bastard. Always the same when you're skint. A ½d. left. What a big-time dog player.

Charles walked over the bridge, stopping about halfway across to gaze upriver.

Wonder what it'd be like falling in, probably wake up in a lovely clean and warm hospital bed with a luscious nurse leaning anxiously over me. Big tits nudging my ears, saying things like 'Would you like a mug of steaming, piping hot coffee, liberally laced with black rum. Also a Player's?'

'Well thank you, wouldn't say no.'

Oh why bother. Come on God, I'm only asking for half a crown. Please make that man in front deaf and blind then let him drop two and six. I promise to take his name and address and send it on to him later.

The rain started falling heavily.

'Who cares,' he shouted waving his fist upwards. 'Who cares anyway eh? My feet are soaking already ha ha ha.'

# He knew him well

The old man lowered the glass from his lips and began rolling another cigarette. His eyes never strayed until finally he lit up inhaling deeply. He stared at me for perhaps thirty seconds then cleared his throat and began speaking. 'Funny places – pubs. Drank in here for near enough thirty years.' He paused shaking his head slowly. 'Never did get to know him. No. Never really spoke to him apart from Evening Jim. Night Jim. Been in the navy. Yes he'd been in the navy all right. Torpedoed I hear. 1944.' He paused again to relight his dead cigarette. 'Only survivor too. Never said much about it. Don't blame him though.' He looked up quickly then peered around the pub. 'No, don't blame him. Talk too much in this place already they do. Never bloody stop, it's no good.' He finished the remainder of his drink and looked over to the bar, catching the barman's eye who nodded, opened a Guinness and sent it across.

'Slate,' said the old guy, 'pay him pension day.' He smiled. 'Not supposed to drink this, says it's bad for me gut – the doctor.'

'Yeah?' I said.

'Oh, yeah,' he nodded, 'yes, said it would kill me if I weren't careful,' looking at me over the top of his spectacles. 'Seventy-two I am, know that. Kill me! Ha! Bloody idiot.'

'Did you like old Jim though?' I asked.

'Well never really knew him did I? I would've though. Yes, I would've liked old Jim if we'd spoke. But we never talked much, him and I. Not really.' He paused for a sip, continued,

'Knew his brother though – a couple of years older than Jim I think. And a real villain he was. Had a nice wife. I used to do the racetracks then and sometimes met Bert there.' The old man stopped again, carefully extracting the long dead roll-up from between his lips and putting it into his waistcoat pocket. He took out his tobacco tin and rolled another. 'Yeah old Bert.' He lit up. 'He was a villain. Used to tell me a few things – yes he did know horses and made a good living. Never came in here except to see old Jim.'

'How did they get on together?' I asked.

'Old Jim and Bert?' He scratched his head. 'Well. Don't know. Didn't say much to each other. Some brothers don't you know,' he was looking over his glasses at me, 'no they'd usually just sit drinking, sometimes laughing. Not talking though. Not much anyway, probably said everything I suppose. Course maybe Jim would ask after Bert's wife and kids or something.'

'Was old Jim never married then?' I asked.

'Maybe he was. Couldn't really say, Guvnor'd tell you.'

'Who, him?' I pointed over to the bartender.

'What, him! Ha.' The old guy snorted into his drink, 'Guvnor'd? He would like that. Bloody guvnor. No his brother-in-law old Jack Moore's the guvnor but he's been laid up now for over a year. Broke his leg and it's never healed up, not properly. Him!' He pointed over to the bar, 'Slag thinks he'll get this place if Jackie packs it in,' the old man's voice was beginning to rise in excitement. 'No chance, no bloody chance of that. Even his sister hates his guts.' He was speaking rather loudly now and I looked to see if the bartender was loitering but he seemed engrossed in cleaning the counter. The old man noticed my concern and leaned across the table. 'Don't pay any attention,' he spoke quietly, 'he hears me alright but he won't let on. Bloody slag. What was I saying though? Old Jim, yes he could drink. Scotch he liked. Drank it all the time. Don't care much for it myself. A drop of rum now and then. That does me.' He paused to roll another cigarette. 'He used to play football. Palace I think or maybe the Orient. Course he was getting on when the war began, just about ready to pack it in then and he never went back afterwards as he lost his arm.'

'Was that in the war?'

'Yes, when he was torpedoed,' the old man was silent for nearly two minutes, puffing at his roll-up between sips of the black rum I'd got him. 'Funny he should have waited so long to do it. Nearly seventy, course maybe his arm had something to do with it.' He scratched his head and said, 'Course they talk in this place. Wouldn't if Jackie was here though. No. Not bloody likely they wouldn't,' he sucked his plastic teeth, 'no not if Jackie was here behind the bar.' He inhaled very deeply. 'Where'd you find him then . . . I mean what like was he when,' the old man stopped and finished his drinks.

'Well,' I said, 'just like it said in the papers. I was a bit worried 'cause I hadn't seen him for a couple of days so I went along and banged his door. No answer, so I went off to the Library to see if I could see him there.'

'The Library?' the old man looked puzzled.

'Yeah, old Jim used to go up before opening time nearly every day.'

'Yes expect he would,' said the old man, 'now I think on it.'

'Anyway,' I continued, 'I got back about half five and saw the landlady. She was worried so I said did she want me to force the door. She said if I thought so I broke the door in and he was lying there, on the bed. The landlady saw him too before I could stop her. Throat sliced open. Doctor said he couldn't have eaten for over a week.'

'Bloody fool,' the old man sighed, 'he should've ate. That's one thing you should do is eat. I eat every day. Yes, make sure of that. Well you've got to. Plate of soup's good you know.'

I had ordered two drinks just on the last bell, we stayed silent, smoking and drinking until I finished and rose and said to him, 'Well old man I'm off. See you again.'

'Yes,' he said staring into his glass shaking his head, 'old Jim should've ate eh!'

# The Last Night

When Pete arrived home, well after midnight, the camp was in complete darkness. Fortunately the long dry spell had made the walk across the field comparatively safe. During the earlier part of the month the field had been reduced to a swamp and Pete had had to remove his socks, if he was wearing any, when crossing. One night when drunk, he had fallen full length into a cowbog and had to have a fully clothed shower afterwards.

The gate creaked as he closed it behind him. He walked noiselessly to his tent and fumbled around inside for his toilet bag and towel. He still felt rather pissed, a shower would freshen him up. A transistor sounded out from a nearby tent. As he walked to the washroom he hummed along with the singer.

There were two shower cubicles and each had a sixpenny slot attached to the door. However Pete had a steel comb which he surreptitiously used to force the lock when no one was around. He decided to brush his teeth first and as he squeezed the paste onto the toothbrush the door opened.

He watched in the mirror.

'Hullo there,' he said, vaguely recognizing one of the holidaymakers, a lad of about eighteen.

'Hullo,' replied the youth, 'didn't think there'd be anyone about.' He had a towel round his shoulders.

'Oh, I just got back,' grinned Pete into the mirror.

'Have you?' he asked enviously, 'Were you in St Helier?'

'Yeah, I was in over the weekend. Drank too much as usual. Pubs are too good in this place.'

Pete began brushing his teeth.

'Too hot to sleep,' said the youth, 'I was going to have a swim.'

'Christ Almighty!' Pete spat into the basin. 'You kidding?'

'No! I was in last night.'

'But the pool's covered with drowned flies.'

'I never noticed.'

'Must be crackers man.' Pete rinsed his mouth. 'Anyway,' he continued, 'I'm going for a shower, a hot one.'

Pete walked to the cubicle door.

'Now don't watch,' he said, pulling out his steel comb.

The youth smiled as Pete inserted it in between the lock and the door.

'Do you do that too?' he asked.

'What! It was me who started it son. Holidaymakers should have more respect.' He grinned.

'Imagine charging sixpence for a shower though.'

'Yeah it's pretty stiff. What's your name?'

'Dave, Dave.'

'Well, I'm Pete. See you later.' He stepped inside and closed the door behind him.

Dave heard the tap being turned on as he left the washroom. The moon cast light over the campsite now, and the stars were glittering.

He opened the small gate leading to the pool. There were no flies as far as he could see. Throwing off his jumper and jeans he took a deep breath and plunged straight in. The water was colder than the previous night. He swam two lengths before jumping out shivering. Collecting his clothes and towel, he ran back to the washroom to dry.

Pete was combing his hair when he entered. Cold beads of water stood out on the boy's goose-pimpled body.

'Christ Almighty! Don't shake near me man.'

'Fresh and invigorating,' laughed Dave, 'very healthy.'

'Crackers, I wouldn't swim in there in the middle of a heat-wave.'

'Why not?' asked Dave rubbing himself down.

'It's not been cleaned for two months. Can you imagine all those kids in there peeing and throwing lumps of mud about. And what about the drowned flies for God's sake.'

Pete pulled out a packet of cigarettes.

'Here,' he offered the packet.

Dave accepted one and finished dressing.

'How long you been here Dave?'

'Almost two weeks. Go back day after tomorrow.'

'Like it?' asked Pete sitting himself on the washhand basin.

'Not bad. Saw nearly everything. Went to the old German hospital yesterday and we went around the island again today.'

'More than I've done in four months.'

'Four months?' echoed Dave.

'Yeah, I'm doing the season. My fourth,' he added.

'Lucky man,' murmured Dave.

'Yeah, it's a good place this.'

'Is the old Irishman with you?'

'Old Patrick?' Pete smiled, 'he isn't with anybody.'

'What do you do to live?'

'Oh picking. Potatoes, tomatoes, strawberries, roses.' Pete shrugged. 'Pick anything at all. Even noses.'

He jumped down from the basin.

'Anyway Dave I start work in approximately six hours.' He opened the door, 'See you tomorrow if you're around.'

At 7.15 a.m. Pete wearily stretched out an arm from the sleeping bag and switched off the alarm. He dragged himself out, pulled on his patched jeans and tee shirt then slipped into his sandals. The farmer's boy had left the carton of milk under the outside flap. Even this early in the morning the temperature was soaring near 70°F. Pete drank half and hid the remainder in the long damp grass near his tent to stay fresh, covered by a polythene bag to ward off insects.

One or two campers were already up, the men out for a bit of peace before the children took over. The washroom was busy and Pete had to queue for an empty basin. Come August and it would be like Portobello Road on a Saturday afternoon. Some of the men were talking to each other, gingerly using christian names.

Pete was allowed a basin by one of the men before his turn. He was accorded some respect because of his status as a seasonal worker.

Among the hundred or so people camping on the site there were only two working the season. The previous year there had been eight but this season only Pete had returned with the old Irishman. Patrick had first come during the late fifties for some mysterious reason. Pete had guessed at tax problems but he was a close man and gave no clue whatsoever. He had come back every year since then only returning to Sligo every Christmas to visit his family and hand in all his money. Pete had come four seasons ago and had no fixed plans. He was twenty-four now and returned to London for four months each year. It was becoming more of a wrench to leave Jersey with every winter. However he had no fixed plans.

Patrick and he had remained close friends after sharing a pot of vegetable soup for four days when both men were without money or work at the beginning of Pete's second season.

As Pete washed his face he was aware of a heavy smell drifting from the cubicles. Noticing two or three holidaymakers with wrinkled noses looking self-consciously about the room, he smiled inwardly.

A door clanged shut and old Patrick appeared, book in one hand. The other held his stomach.

'Ah Jasus me guts.' He shook his head mournfully as he crossed the damp floor.

'You're late,' said Pete who was drying his neck.

'Twenty-five minutes in the shit house? No bloody wonder boy.' The old man stopped, 'Where've you been the last couple o' days?'

'In town.'

'Boy,' said Patrick, 'you'll have no chopper left if you don't slow down.' Pete smiled following him from the washroom. The sun was streaming down. Old Patrick pulled his ancient bunnet down over his red, gnarled face.

'Good Christ what a heat. Blind a man,' he muttered as they walked to their tents.

'Could have done well last night if you'd been in,' he continued. 'Plenty tourists about.'

'I'll be in tonight,' said Pete, 'although I'm pretty broke.'

'Did you get a bit when you were in?'

Pete shrugged, 'I'm saying nothing.'

The old Irishman snorted.

'Don't want to get you all worked up man,' Pete said. 'You might rape a cow or something.'

'Ha!' cried Patrick, 'don't worry about me boy. I don't go short. Don't worry about that.' Pete burst into laughter and flicked his towel at him.

'See you later you lying old bastard,' he shouted.

'Aye,' called Patrick as they parted, 'and you'd better bring some money 'cause I'm buying you nothing.'

They worked on different farms. Patrick drove a tractor for John Fasquelle down at St Martin and Pete worked near Grouville for Freddie Coffier. He cycled the three miles there and back on a ramshackle bicycle Coffier had given him. He was a good boss and Pete made his own hours, normally working from eight until five unless they were exceptionally busy. He was paid 6/6 an hour tax free and the farmer paid all his insurance.

Pete arrived home after five and boiled some freshly picked potatoes which he had with a frozen minute steak and the remaining half pint of milk. Some holidaymakers were eating dinner and a few were recuperating in the sun, dozing to Radio 1. Pete ate quickly then carried the dirty utensils to the washroom.

'Hullo there.'

Pete stopped, seeing Dave approach.

'Hullo Dave how are you doing?'

'Okay. How was work?'

'Too hot,' Pete answered, 'far too hot man.'

'What are you doing now? I mean after, where are you going?'

'I'll be off for a few pints.'

'To St Helier?'

'No. Just down to the cross.'

'The hotel?'

'Yeah. The Queen's. Fancy coming along?'

'Yes,' Dave looked pleased, 'how long will you be?'

'As soon as I do this lot,' he looked at the utensils. 'Ten minutes.'

'Okay, I'll go and get changed.' Dave turned and walked off.

About twenty minutes later they met at the gate entrance to the campsite. Pete grinned to himself when Dave appeared wearing a suit and a shirt and tie.

'Kind of formal man,' he said. 'The locals will take you for a tourist.'

'Well it's a hotel,' he hesitated. 'Oh who cares. I am a tourist anyway.'

Pete laughed, 'I doubt if Patrick'll even talk to you.'

'The old Irishman?' asked Dave.

Pete nodded. 'Yes. The best domino man on the Channel Islands.'

'Oh!' Dave glanced sideways at him.

The Queen's Hotel stood at the crossroads just under a two-mile walk from the campsite. It had a bar, a lounge and a fair-sized restaurant all of which opened seven days a week to resident and non-resident alike. The lounge was patronized by holidaymakers and wealthy retired couples in contrast to the large bar where the local farmworkers congregated. They were in the main Bretons and tended to drink in one large group by the bar. A few tourist husbands on the run from television lounges would end up here where they could have a quiet pint and perhaps a game of darts or dominoes.

When Pete and Dave entered the bar the Irishman was sitting near the group of Frenchmen, chatting to an old crony who puffed on a gray clay pipe. Pete asked Dave what he wanted to drink.

'Pint of bitter and a pint of Guinness, Sam,' called Pete to the barman.

He turned to Dave.

'Notice how he never acknowledged it?'

Dave nodded.

'That's because I haven't been in for two days. They think if you're not here you must be in some other boozer spending the money.'

'But you were,' replied Dave grinning.

'That's not the point though.' He shrugged, 'What's the difference?'

They carried their drinks to a table not far from the jukebox. Dave played three records and when he run on Pete said, 'What do you do for a living man?'

'I go up to University at the beginning of September.'

'Very good,' replied Pete seriously. 'What do you intend doing afterwards?'

'I've no idea,' he shrugged, 'teach maybe. I don't really know.'

'Your parents want you to be a teacher?'

'My mother does,' he grinned wryly. 'My father doesn't care as long as I use my qualifications.'

Pete finished his pint and Dave rose, downing the dregs of his.

'Same again?' he asked.

Pete nodded and he walked to the bar to order. Pete sat back in his chair looking around the crowded room. He saw Patrick receiving a fresh pint at the bar. He waved and the old man strolled across the room.

'Been in long?'

'Half past four. I finished early.' He gazed around the room, still standing holding his pint of Guinness. He smiled down at Pete and jerked his head.

'Think we could get a game going boy. I'll get the doms.'

'By the way Patrick, there's a young guy with me.'

'Aye, I saw him.'

'He's camping with his parents up at the site.'

'Is he now?'

'Yeah, he's okay.'

Patrick nodded and left for the bar as Dave returned with his round.

'Do you play dominoes?' asked Pete.

'No, not really. Not since I was a kid.'

'Well listen,' he leaned across, 'me and old Patrick usually get a game going.'

Dave nodded with the glimmer of a smile.

'Partners you know? Just for pints,' he grinned, 'with the tourists.'

'I see,' Dave grinned back, 'you mean you con them.'

'Well we don't really con them man, I mean they enjoy the game and once or twice we have been known to pay for an evening.'

'Not very often though.'

'Once or twice.'

'In four years.' Dave laughed, 'I'll enjoy watching.'

'Right,' said Pete.

Patrick came back with the domino box and board. Pete spread the pieces face down and shuffled.

'Quick game of knockout eh? Miserable shillings OK?'

'Does he know the game well enough?' Patrick gestured vaguely towards Dave.

'Enough to lose a couple of bob,' Pete winked at Dave.

'Looks like he's going to the bloody dancing,' grunted the Irishman.

They settled down to the game, playing steadily for half an hour before one man who had been spectating for two games asked if he could have a hand. Pete said yes and the fellow sat in. He was a Newcastle man and said his name was John and his mate who liked a game would be in in ten minutes. His mate duly arrived and was invited in.

'If you don't mind I'll just watch,' said Dave moving to another seat.

Old Patrick shrugged, 'Fancy partners?'

'Aye,' said John, 'mates. Fancy it Bert? Me and you eh? The old firm.'

'Aye good idea Johnnie.' Bert turned to the other two, 'Half pints a corner eh?'

The two friends were on holiday with their wives and they were boarding together in a small hotel near St Martin.

After a comment on the weather the dominoes were shuffled and the men lifted six apiece.

'Heh, heh. Is this what starts the game off then?' asked John laying the double six on the board.

Pete smiled at him, Bert made no sign. Old Patrick farted loudly. The big game was under way.

Dave watched the first few games but soon lost interest apart from when he had to go to the bar for the losers' rounds. After a while the stakes were raised to pints then eventually to shorts. Patrick and Pete were winning consistently now and Dave was being pushed an occasional whisky from Pete.

The bar was crowded now and a group of young men and women in yachting gear were standing by the counter drinking half pints of mild and trying to engage the French farmworkers in conversation. There were cries of 'Oui' now and then, and an occasional 'Oo la la' as one of the older Bretons slapped one of the young English women on the bum. Everyone was laughing and enjoying the fun.

About thirty minutes before closing time, Bert stood up after another defeat and sniffed.

'Think I'll turn in now. What about you John eh? Coming?'

'Aye,' replied John rising to his feet, 'long day ahead of us tomorrow.'

'Okay lads, good game,' said Pete.

'Not a bad game eh?' John asked Patrick.

'Played worse,' agreed the old Irishman.

'Aye!' Bert smiled at last, 'aye you're too hot for us, lads. Come on mate,' he emphasized the last word as he led his friend from the bar.

'He wasn't a bad player,' said Pete.

'Aye,' Patrick nodded. 'Don't know where he found his friend though.'

Dave yawned, 'What time do they close?'

'About ten past eleven,' replied Pete. 'Think I've had enough myself. What about you Patrick?'

'Think I'll stay on for a few minutes.'

Dave stood up unsteadily holding on to the table.

'Good night.' Patrick knocked his pipe out and began cutting from a block of moist black tobacco. 'Better take the boy home Pete,' he grunted out the corner of his mouth.

Pete nodded and steadied Dave as they walked to the exit.

The path leading between the fields from the cross to the camp site had no lighting of any kind and when Pete had first come to the island courage had to be taken to walk home alone. Now being accustomed to the country he never gave the darkness a second thought.

Shortly after leaving the hotel Dave staggered up to a tree where he spewed and retched for a while. Pete was rather worried about any possible reaction from his parents. Bad examples, corrupting influences, etc. Still Dave was old enough to take care of himself.

'Man you look really awful,' said Pete sympathetically.

'Oh God!' Dave closed his eyes, both hands supported by the tree, he shuddered fitfully.

Later Pete asked him if he was able to continue the walk home.

'Think so,' mumbled Dave. 'Feel bit better.'

'Fine,' said Pete pulling out a packet of cigarettes, 'want a fag?'

'No, no,' groaned Dave shaking his head violently.

'Okay, okay, sorry,' said Pete quickly, adding, 'come on, we better start or we'll be here all night.'

He strode on and Dave lurched steadfastly after him. Ten minutes had passed before Pete stopped. He said, 'Have to have a piss. You carry on man and I'll catch you up.'

Dave nodded silently and staggered on up the track disappearing into the night.

Pete finished and lighted a cigarette feeling surprisingly well. Perhaps watching Dave had helped sober him up. Poor bastard. He hitched up his jeans and set off after him walking quickly. Probably find him lying in a ditch somewhere, good suit and all.

'Ah! Aaah.'

A terrible cry rent the still night from a hundred yards ahead.

'Ah God! Aaa.'

Pete stopped in his tracks. 'Christ Almighty,' he said loudly.

He heard the sound of running footsteps increasing in volume then Dave burst into view sprinting madly.

'Up there,' he gasped. 'Up there in the middle of the road.'

Pete looked and could see nothing. Dave tugged his arm.

'Come on,' he cried, 'come on.'

'Wait a minute,' shouted Pete.

But too late. Dave was away and practically out of sight on his way back to the hotel.

As Pete stood wondering what to do old Patrick approached hurriedly.

'Hoy Pete, what's up with the kid? Nearly knocked me over the bloody fool.'

'God knows Patrick. Something in the middle of the road.'

'Aye he said something like that. Come on. Let's find out.'

They set off walking side by side in case of emergencies, although neither admitted as much. Pete was whistling uneasily while Patrick's pipe-stem seemed to be about to snap due to the pressure exerted on it by his false teeth.

As they turned a bend in the path they could vaguely make out a dark shape filling the pathway.

'Jesus!' Pete moved one pace forward and laughed with relief.

'A cow!' he said, 'It's a bloody cow.'

'A bloody *old* cow,' answered Patrick in disgust. 'Just what you'd expect. You better go and find that boy.'

'What about you? You not coming?'

'Me?' the old man snorted, 'see you tomorrow boy.'

'You rotten old bastard,' said Pete grinning.

'Bloody dancing he should've been, that's what. Eh? Bloody dancing.'

Patrick laughed and lighted his pipe then, giving a wave, ambled on home.

Pete watched him go then turned and set off to discover whether Dave had reached St Helier.

# Wednesday

'Jimmy! Jimmy! Come on, it's half past.'

'What? What is it?'

Billy was leaning over me shaking my shoulder. 'Half past five man come on.'

'I'm not going.' I closed my eyes as I realised today was Wednesday. Day before pay day. We had no money. No food. No cigarettes. Nothing at all. 'I'm not going man.'

'You're daft you bastard.' Billy looked disgusted. 'What's the point in staying here? There's no grub. Nothing. Might get a tap in work.'

I opened my eyes. 'It's raining.'

'So you're not going?' He put on his jacket.

'No sir. No sirree. Tell old Dick. Oh tell him anything at all.'

Billy opened the door and looked around. 'You tell him tomorrow.'

'OK.' I pulled the blankets up to my chin. 'Christ it's really terrible in here. So cosy and warm. Oh it's really bad. I wish I could go to work. You're lucky.'

'Aye I know,' he looked angry, 'I'm getting a new place Jimmy, this is hopeless.'

'Oh no,' I mumbled sleepily.

The door slammed as I turned over.

About 10.30 a.m. I awoke with a clear conscience and began searching for food. Billy and I had looked everywhere last night but unknown to him I had found an egg which I had secreted among the old ash in the fireplace. I looked elsewhere for something more but found nothing.

I washed the egg before breaking the shell and emptying it into the frying pan. Then I realized I should have boiled it. Too late now. One fried egg for breakfast. Still there were three or four tea leaves left and enough dust to make at least one cup of tea. No milk though. I noticed the old empty tin of Carnation lying on top of the rubbish box. Yes! I could pour some boiling water into it and swirl it about. Enough for a cup. Things were looking better.

I switched on the kettle and turned on the electric ring before returning to the room to make the bed and tidy up a bit. There was a chance of finding a dowt somewhere. Perhaps in the fireplace? Billy had looked there last night though. Not much hope. I searched around for a while before discovering the large butt of a Capstan under the carpet. That sneaky bastard! He must have tapped it from a lodger. Well, well, well. What a dirty bastard. I thought I smelled smoke this morning. What! Something up! The kettle had not whistled.

I put the dowt behind my ear and walked through to the kitchen. The switch! Electricity! The slot! Jesus no shilling. No breakfast. Overcome with despair I sat down, close to tears. My mind was completely blank for some time. Then. Raw eggs! Very healthy. Yes and there was some Yorkshire relish to mix in.

'Hullo there!' I cried for joy and jumping to my feet ran through to the kitchen where I spooned the egg from the frying pan up into a cup. I took the sauce bottle down from the shelf and laid it on the sink, then drank some ice-cold water, straight from the tap. Ah, even Manchester water is so refreshing.

I grabbed the bottle and shook the liquid into the cup. Closing my eyes I raised the cup to my lips and drank half. Immediately I spluttered and coughed and spewed into the sink. Groaning I bent my head down between my knees realising what I had done. I could still taste it. My God I had picked up the Fairy Liquid instead of the Yorkshire Relish. I straightened and turned on the tap to wash away the breakfast. Something attracted my attention. The ultimate piece of all the bad luck which had ever befallen me. The cigarette butt had fallen from my ear and was now soggily floating with the tide of green-coloured yolk towards the drain.

I staggered into the room and collapsed onto the bed a raving maniac. Somehow I must have undressed and crawled under the blankets, as the next thing I knew, the door had opened and the landlady's cleaner was staring down at me. She held a broom and shovel in one hand.

'Sorry, thought you were at work. Always do in here Wednesdays.'

'That's OK.' I sat up, 'If you start in the kitchen I'll get up.'

'You don't have to.'

'No, I was about to get up anyway.'

'All right then.'

She walked through to the kitchen closing the door behind her.

I dressed quickly, rather embarrassed as she had noticed my clothes strewn around the room and my underwear had not been changed for a fortnight although I doubt whether she had noticed that.

'OK?'

'Yes,' I answered.

The kitchen door opened and she peeped around, 'Somebody been sick in here?'

I nodded, 'Bad stomach, that's why I didn't go in to work.'

'Ah there's a germ going the rounds.' She returned to her duties.

I picked up a book and sat down. I could not concentrate, my mind was on food and my orchestral stomach began tuning up. Ten minutes elapsed then on impulse I rose and opened the kitchen door.

'Fancy some tea?' I asked.

'Please.'

'Fine, I'll just go and wash first.'

I retreated quickly to the communal bathroom hoping for a miracle. I sat meditating on what to say when I returned. In all I must have had about a dozen different replies ready for her possible questions.

When I eventually got back to the flat I found the cleaner had left; however, her tools were still lying on the kitchen floor. God what could I say to her? All my answers sounded ridiculous. Suddenly the door opened and she entered carrying a shopping bag.

'Here.' She passed me a single shilling which I accepted silently and slid into the slot.

'You remind me of my son and my man.' She smiled faintly, 'and my father and brothers.'

I stood saying nothing.

'You tidy up the room and I'll make the tea,' she said.

'Thanks.'

With some relief I watched her go into the kitchen. I set to making the bed again. My nose was going mad. Just as I had finished cleaning out the fireplace the door opened and she came through carrying a tray. There was a plate straining under a pile of buttered toast and another two, each containing three sausages, an egg, beans and a fried potato scone.

'I'm hungry too,' she said with the glimmer of a smile, placing the tray on the table. 'Sit down and I'll bring in the tea.'

A morning paper could be the only other thing I desired at that moment. When we finished the meal she gathered up the plates and I sat back with the book. She reappeared five minutes later with her bag and tools.

'Thanks an awful lot missus. You saved my life there, you really did.'

'Time you got married,' she commented, leaving the room.

A great woman. Truly great.

I returned to my book aware of the rain still battering down outside. It was pathetic. A typically dismal day before pay day. The only possible way to be happy on a day such as this would be to have your insurance cards, two weeks' wages plus holiday money and a ticket to London.

I could not concentrate on my book. Would it be possible to nip the landlady? I mean Christ, I paid two weeks in advance and there's a tenner deposit on top of that. Surely one miserable pound would be forthcoming! Eh?

An hour had passed before I had plucked up the necessary courage to descend to her office. If she refused I could threaten her. Tell her I'd shop her to the busies for allowing brass nails on the premises. And she must be getting something for it! No doubt about that.

Yes I would see her. First I had to go for a shit, the combination of egg and beans was deadly. I left the flat and as I descended the flight of stairs leading to the toilet the door opened and one of the aforementioned ladies came out. She smiled demurely, brushing by me in a loose floral dressing gown. She smelled good.

'Good morning,' I called after her.

Prospects there if I ever won a few quid on the horses.

As I sat with my trousers around my ankles, hunched over reading an ancient copy of the *People's Friend* which had been placed on the newly washed linoleum, I noticed a £1 note lying near the washhand basin. I continued reading aware of the blood pounding through my temples then I closed my eyes and opened them slowly. Good God Almighty it still lay there with the green lady winking up at me. Struck constipated I pulled up my trousers and pounced upon it. I silently half opened the door peering around. No one! I stole up the stairs and tiptoed into my flat.

'Hullo there! Hullo you good thing.' I burst out laughing and threw myself on the bed holding the pound note in the air. Guilt! Guilt pangs? That girl's hard-earned bread. Who are you kidding man, handful for a short time? Jesting! Might not even be hers. Could be the cleaner's? Christ it gets worse. No! Must be the girl's. Girl? Must be near thirty man. Anyway.

I lay back staring at the ceiling. When she finds out she'll know it's me. Suss that out right away. Well, well, well. Some thief. Some bloody thief right enough.

I stood up and decided to return it immediately. Anonymously would be best. I crept along the corridor and quietly inserted it in her letter box then I returned to the lavatory and resumed where I had left off.

About half an hour later, back in my flat, I had managed to get involved in the book when there came a knock on the door. I opened.

'Hullo,' she was still wearing the floral dressing gown. 'Did you find this?' she asked, holding the pound note out.

I nodded and blushed.

'Here,' she smiled handing me a ten bob piece, 'thanks a lot.'

'No!' I shouted, 'No thanks, that's all right,' mumbling now. 'You sure?'

'Yeah. I'm OK. Yes thanks.' My neck was beginning to ache with the amount of nodding my head was doing.

'Well if you're sure,' she smiled seriously. 'Thanks very much.'

I closed the door still nodding my red head. What a stupid bastard. I lay back on the bed utterly spent. Ten bob. Not even a fag. I jumped to my feet, opened the door and marched down the corridor. I knocked loudly on her door. It opened almost immediately.

'Have you a cigarette to spare,' I faltered then added lamely, 'Don't have any. None at all.'

She smiled, 'You should have said. Come in.'

I entered. A man stood by the far window watching quietly. An older woman sat on the settee with a drink in one hand.

'What's your name?' the girl asked.

'Jimmy.' I nodded, 'Jimmy.'

She turned and introduced me. The man smiled pleasantly remaining silent, he was over six feet tall but kind of thin.

'Jimmy found the pound,' she looked at me quite proudly, 'I'm Joan; Alice, pour him a sherry.'

I accepted the drink to be sociable and Joan gave me a Rothman King Size, motioning me to take a seat on the long settee.

'Well girls,' the tall man crossed the room, 'that's settled then?'

Joan shrugged, 'If you like.'

Alice gestured from the settee with her sherry glass, muttering to herself. Frowning, he made as if to say something, changed his mind and left.

The door had barely closed when Alice snorted loudly, 'Good bloody riddance!' I half expected him to come back. He must have heard her. 'I don't know Joanie,' Alice continued, 'I really don't. He expects too much. Far too much.' She looked across at me. 'Too bloody much. So he does.' I sipped the sherry. Never seen the bloke before and yet he had to be the pimp. 'Anyway,' Alice stood up and drained her glass, 'I'm off to do some shopping.' Joan yawned as she lifted the bottle of sherry.

'OK, Alice,' she said, leaning over and topping up my glass.

'Cheerio,' I said.

'Bye lad,' replied Alice staring at me.

The door closed behind her and I sat back enjoying the drink and smoke.

'Is she at it too?' I asked.

Joan nodded with big eyes.

'Is she not a bit old?' Good God what a ridiculous question.

'Too old for what?' she smiled at me, 'Alice isn't even forty.'

'She should be settled down by now,' I said by way of an explanation.

'She was married. Three kids as well. She left them all about two years ago,' Joan walked to the sink. 'Coffee?'

'Yes thanks,' I answered, 'Where'd you meet her?'

Joan busied around the oven for two or three minutes and I was beginning to think she had not heard. Then she turned mock dramatically.

'She's my auntie.'

'Your auntie?'

She burst into laughter at the expression on my face.

'Do you want to hear a sob story?'

I held out my glass for a refill. 'Not particularly.'

'Just as well, don't know any anyway.' Joan came over and sat facing me. I thought she had been wearing a bra earlier. Must have been mistaken.

'He's gay.'

'What?'

'Him!' she pointed to the door. 'He's bent.'

'Oh!' I was surprised. 'Are you sure?'

She looked at me like I was daft or something.

'Did you not notice?'

'Well it crossed my mind.'

'Bloody liar.' She was laughing at me again.

'Well sometimes it's difficult to tell.'

'That's probably why he rushed away,' she continued.

'Why?'

'Jealous. That's why.'

'Ha ha ha,' I said finishing the drink to cover my blushes.

'No,' she said, 'Young fellow like you.'

'Good stuff this,' I waved to the bottle playing for time.

'Home brew,' she poured me another. 'Never mind that label, it's very potent stuff.'

'Aphrodisiac qualities?' I laughed half heartedly. 'I mean has it? Eh?'

'Alice made it so it's very possible,' she said pouring herself one.

'Randy old bugger she is. You want to watch her too.'

The kettle shrilled and she walked over to the cooker.

'Still want some coffee?'

'No, not for me, thanks,' I replied.

Standing with her back to me for a few moments, she switched off the gas, absentmindedly it seemed.

'Nice of you to return that pound. Don't suppose you've got any money either.'

'Well it's pay day tomorrow,' I explained.

Old Alice's brew was beginning to take a hold of me.

Wonder what she put in it? I poured myself another.

'Like it?' asked Joan sitting back down on the settee.

I nodded and passed her one of her cigarettes, taking one myself. My hand was shaking uncontrollably as I reached across to give her a light.

'All right?' she asked behind those big, big eyes.

'Whoo I'm okay. Powerful stuff that stuff.'

My hand was not shaking because of the bloody drink. No, no, no! Her dressing gown had opened almost down to her waist as she leaned forward to light up. What a pair of tits she had on her!

'You have a fine pair of, eh! breasts there, Joan. You really have.'

'Thanks but they are a bit small.'

'What are you talking about? Whoo they're perfect.'

She smiled gracefully.

I placed my glass carefully on the carpet and as I leaned across to her, knocked it over.

'Don't mind it,' said Joan, 'just leave it lying.'

Her gown lay precariously round her shoulders, she jerked forward slightly and it fell on to the cushions behind her.

I placed a forefinger on each of her nipples feeling remarkably fine for a Wednesday.

# Dinner for Two

By the time he had found his front door key, Mr Joranski the landlord approached carrying a bag of groceries.

'Well Charles,' he asked, 'get paid?'

'Yes John, I'll be able to give you three weeks.'

'What?' Mr Joranski was astonished.

'They gave me a tenner for some reason.'

'Very nice. Very nice. You want some food?'

Charles nodded, 'Yes. Great, I'll be down in a minute.'

Mr Joranski departed to the basement and Charles climbed the steep stairs leading to his room on the third floor. He changed into his best trousers and jumper and pulled on his newly purchased black socks.

By the time he had reached the basement the landlord had the table set and the meal almost ready.

The basement consisted of a communal sitting room with a television, an old decrepit couch and odd chairs dotted around the walls. One enormous peculiar table lay propped against one wall. Everything from poker games to shove halfpenny took place on this table. If there were unexpected guests or perhaps a big game on at Wembley every bed and chair in the house would be occupied and the landlord would throw a blanket on his table and sleep there himself. He had been a soldier. Rumour had it he had carried this table all the way from Warsaw through two concentration camps, walked across Europe, come by rowing boat to Aberdeen and from there hitchhiked his way to King's Cross. No one could understand how he had managed to get it down the basement stairs and through the narrow sitting-room door.

'Sure you can afford it?' he asked as Charles gave him nine singles. 'Nine quid from ten leaves one you know?'

'Take it quickly man.'

'Okay.' Mr Joranski smiled, 'You want to borrow anything later just come down. Not too much though or we're back to the beginning again, all right?'

'Bring on the grub John,' said Charles.

'Yes, yes bring on the grub. I have good sausage Polish!' He shook his head. 'German no good, Hungarian not too bad. Polish?' he smacked his lips. 'Mmmm. Here cut some bread.'

Charles sliced through the thick crusty loaf.

'Any butter?' he asked.

'Butter?' echoed John, 'Of course butter. What do you think?'

He pulled a packet from his provision bag. The kettle whistled from the kitchen. John rose.

'I go make some tea.'

Charles buttered a few thick slices of bread and cut some chunks of blue cheese. The landlord returned in a matter of moments with two odd mugs of tea.

'I'm starving John,' said Charles.

'You should eat more,' he poured some condensed milk into the mugs of tea. 'Sugar?' he inquired.

'No! Good God!' Charles shook his head. 'It'll taste like tablet. Christ knows how you've a tooth left in your head.'

'Good for you,' replied John. 'Cream and sugar. Kill the taste of this lousy tea. Bloody English tea.' He snorted contemptuously, 'Ugh, lousy lousy.'

'British tea,' corrected Charles out of habit. 'Why d'you buy the stuff then?'

'Who knows?' The landlord bit off a chunk of bread and munched happily.

'John,' said Charles, 'this is the finest sausage I've ever tasted.'

'Back home,' replied John, mouth filled with salami, 'back home this is only average.' He drank some tea. 'Charles you should go to my country sometime. Food!' his eyes widened. 'Ha! In England you oil the machine that right?'

'Don't talk with your mouth full man. You remind me of old Jackson up the stair,' said Charles.

'He pay me every Wednesday. Every Wednesday never misses.'

'What's that got to do with his eating habits? Every time I talk to him when we're eating I can't see my tea for his dinner floating around in my cup.'

'Ah plenty rent no manners,' the landlord shrugged his shoulders, 'How bad?'

'You are all business John, all business,' Charles shook his head slowly.

'All business!' cried the landlord. 'All business? Eat my sausage and pay me nothing.' Joranski jumped to his feet. 'You shout business to me!'

'Take it easy man.'

'Easy? If I'm business you'd be in Euston Station, dossing with dossers. Come on get more tea Scotchman.'

'Get it yourself you immigrant bastard,' answered Charles in anger.

'Immigrant bastard?' repeated John. 'Get the tea! Get a job! Comb your hair and get it cut and a bath. Come on get some rent money for me,' he bellowed pounding his chest with a slice of bread.

'Just gave you nine quid man. What you on about?'

'Fifteen I want. Five weeks at three is fifteen plus two and six for this food.' John thumped his table and sat down. 'You think I'm daft Scotchman. You come and tap me for the money by Sunday morning I know.'

'You just told me to ask if I needed it for God's sake.'

'I'm a bloody fool,' he whacked his forehead with his hand. 'Right Scotchman I get the tea.' He stood up again.

'That's okay John,' Charles got to his feet, 'I'll go for it.'

'Sit!' bawled the landlord, brandishing the bread knife. 'I cut your bloody head off.'

'Okay you get the bloody tea then,' Charles sat down.

'Lazy lazy dossing Scotch bastard. Come on why don't you go home?'

'This is my home, Joranski. Thought you were getting the tea Daddy?'

The landlord snorted, 'My son would not be like you.'

He went through to the kitchen and returned with the teapot.

'No,' he continued, 'I throw him out if he is like you.'

Charles said nothing.

'Come on. Take some more sausage. Plenty cheese.'

'Thanks.' Charles cut a slice and passed it to John.

The landlord bit a chunk and grinned, 'Old Jackson won't eat sausage. I offer him many times but he says no. Garlic.'

'Yeah garlic,' agreed Charles, 'course he's English.'

'Yeah,' nodded John, 'he's English.'

Both men finished and began clearing the table.

'Well?' asked Mr Joranski, 'You going to buy me some beer now?'

'Okay! With pleasure. Come.'

# An old pub near the Angel

Charles wakened at 9.30 a.m. and wasted no time in dressing. Good God it's about time for spring surely. Colder than it was yesterday though and I'll have to wash and shave today. Must. The face has yellow lines. I can't wear socks today. Impossibility. People notice smells although they say nothing.

Think I will do a moonlight tonight, I mean five weeks' rent? He has cause for complaint. Humanity. A touch of humanity is required. He has fourteen tenants paying around £3.00 each for those poxy wee rooms, surely he can afford to let me off paying once in a while. One of his longest-serving tenants. Man I've even been known to clean my room on occasion with no thought of rent reduction.

Still he did take me for a meal last night. Collapsed if he hadn't. Imagine that bloody hotel porter knocking me back. Where's your uniform? Are you a washer up? Those people depress me. What's the difference, one meal more or less? I wonder what it is with them? Old John though – what can I say – after the bollicking he gives me for not trying to get a job and some bread together, who expects him to come back thirty minutes later saying, 'Okay you Scotch dosser. Come and eat,' what could I say apart from, 'Fancy a pint first John?' Yes he has too many good points. Suppose I could give him a week's money. Depends on what they give me though. Anyway.

Charles left the house and made his way towards the Labour Exchange up near Pentonville Road. It was a twenty-five minute walk but one Charles did not mind at all as he normally received six and a half from the NAB for his trouble afterwards.

Yes spring is definitely around the corner man. Look at that briefcase with the sports jacket and cavalry twill slacks. Already? Very daring. Must be a traveller. Best part of the day this – seeing all the workers – office and site and the new middle-class tradesmen all going about their business. It pleases me.

Can't say I'm in the mood for a long wait in the NAB after-wards. Jesus Christ I forgot a book. Man man what do I do now? Borrow newspapers? Stare at people's necks and make goo goos at their children? Good God! The money will be well earned today.

Charles stopped outside the Easy Eats Cafe and breathed in deeply. This fellow must be the best cook in London without any doubt at all. My my my. Every time I pass this place it's the same, smells like bacon and eggs and succulent sausages with toast and tea. Never mind never mind soon be there.

Charles arrived at the Labour Exchange and entered door C. He took up position in the queue under D.

Well I can imagine it today, 'Yes Mr Donald there is some back money owing to you. Would you sign here for £43.68p?' I'd smile politely, 'Oh yes thank you I had been beginning to wonder if it would ever come through. Thank you. Good day.' Then I'd creep out and run like the clappers before they discovered their error. God love us, what's this? What's this noise? Can't be somebody farting in a Labour Exchange. Bloody Irish. Don't understand them at all. Think they delight in embarrassing the English. Everyone kids on they didn't hear it. Surely they can smell it?

Charles stepped out of the queue and tapped the fellow on the shoulder. 'Hoy Mick. That's one helluva smell to make in a public place you know.'

'Ah bejasus,' sighed the Irishman, 'it's that bloody Guinness Jock. Sure I can't help it at all.'

'Terrible stuff for the guts right enough,' said Charles.

'Ah but it's better than that English water they sell here. Bitter?' he shook his head, 'It's a penance to drink it Jock.'

'Aye,' agreed Charles. 'You been waiting long?'

'Not at all,' he shook his head again and spat on the floor. 'Want a roll?'

'You're kidding me Mick?'

'Aw what you going on about? Here,' he took out his pouch and handed it to Charles. 'I've plenty here and I'll be getting a few quid this morning. Help yourself Jock.'

Charles accepted and rolled himself a smoke.

'Been over long, man,' he asked.

'Too long Jock,' he gave a short laugh, 'Still skint.'

He struck a match on the floor and they lit their cigarettes.

'Aye if I'd been buying that Guinness in shares instead of pints I'd be worth a fortune, and that's a fact. The hell with it.'

'You're next Mick,' said Charles.

The Irishman went to the counter and received the signing-on card from the young girl. He signed on and was handed his pay slip then he walked over to the cashier where he received his money and vanished.

Charles followed Mick to the first counter and to his surprise received a pay slip. Normally he got a BI form for the NAB. He asked the girl whether he would still have to visit the Social Security Office.

The girl smiled, 'Not this week anyway Mr Donald.'

Charles strode across to the money counter and stole a quick look at the pay slip. Good God. He looked again.

'God love us,' he said loudly.

£23.82p. Jesus. Oh you good thing. Nearly twenty-four quid. Man man that's almost eighteen back money. What can one say God? Mere words are useless.

He passed the pay slip under the grill to the older lady who dispensed the benefit. She passed him the money after he had signed again.

'My sincere thanks madam,' he said.

The cashier smiled, 'That makes a change.'

'You have a wonderful smile,' continued Charles folding the wad. 'I shall certainly call back here again. Good morning.'

'Good morning,' the cashier watched him back off to the exit.

Charles closed the door. Yes maybe chances there if I followed it through. Maybe she just pities me though, with that smile? Impossible.

He walked up Pentonville Road and decided to go for a pint rather than a breakfast. Ten past eleven. Not too early.

'Pint of bitter and eh. Give me,' Charles stared at the miserable gantry, 'just give me one of your good whiskies eh?'

The ancient barman peered at him for a moment then bent down behind the bar to produce a dusty bottle of Dimple Haig.

'How's this eh?'

'Aye that's fine,' replied Charles. 'How much is it?'

'Seven bob,' the barman muttered rubbing his ear thoughtfully.

'Give me twenty Players too and that's that.'

The barman passed over the cigarettes and grabbed the pound note mumbling to himself. Very friendly old bastard that. Must hate Scotsmen or something. The old man brought back the change and moved around the counter tidying up.

'Hoy!' called Charles after a time. 'Any grub?'

'What's that?' cried the barman left hand at his ear.

'Food! Have you any food?'

'What d'you want eh?'

'Depends. What have you got?'

'Don't know,' he thought for a moment, 'Potato crisps?'

'No chance,' replied Charles. 'Is that it?'

'Shepherd's pie? The wife makes it,' he added smiling strangely.

Wonder why he's smiling like that. Poisoned or something?

'Homemade eh?' asked Charles, 'yeah I'll have some of that.'

'Now?'

'Yes now for heaven's sake,' he shook his head.

'Okay okay, just take a seat and I'll go tell her eh?' He shuffled off. As he passed through the partition he glanced back at Charles who gave him a wave.

Kind of quiet this place. Wonder when it gets busy. Strange I'm the only customer in at eleven thirty on a Thursday morning.

The ancient barman returned.

''Bout ten minutes eh.'

Charles nodded and he resumed wiping some glasses. Charles moved to a table near the window. He lit a cigarette.

Man man who would of thought of me getting back money like that. Brilliant. Let me see. 11.35 a.m. By rights I should still be sitting in the second interview queue at the NAB. The fat woman's kids would be rolling on the floor and she'd be reading the *Evening Standard* dog section. Yes I'll be missed. They'll think I've gone to Scotland. Or maybe been lifted by the busies. Won't have to go back there for a while. Perhaps just as well. I could have ended up in trouble if that sarcastic civil servant bastard had persisted in aggravating me. I would have had to hit him. No choice.

A huge woman appeared from behind the partition holding a plateful of steaming shepherd's pie.

'One shepherd's pie,' she cried.

Her chins trembled and her breasts rested on her knees as she bent to plonk the full plate down in front of Charles' table.

'This looks wonderful,' said he sniffing the meal. He smiled up at her, 'Madam you've excelled yourself. How much do you ask for this delicious fare?'

'14p.' She pointed to her husband. 'He'll give you the condiments. Just shout, he's deaf occasionally.'

'Many thanks,' said Charles placing 20p on her tray. 'Please have a drink on me.'

'Ta son,' she said as she toddled off to the kitchen.

Charles ate quickly and thoroughly enjoyed the meal.

'Hoy! Hoy!' he called when he had finished.

The barman was standing elbows leaning on the counter, staring up at the blank television screen.

'Hoy!' shouted Charles again, walking to the bar.

'Yeah? Yeah? What up eh?'

'Another pint of bitter and have one yourself.'

'What's that?'

'Jesus! What's up here at all. Listen man. Get me a pint of bitter please and have one with me eh? How's that eh?' cried Charles.

'Fine son, I'll have a half. Nice weather eh?' the old fellow pulled the drinks showing distinct signs of energy.

'Pity about the Fulham eh? Still they'll be back, the old Fulham eh? Yeah they'll be back eh?' He took a long swig of beer. Eyes closed, a slow stream trickled down his half-shaven chin winding its way round his Adam's apple on down under his shirt collar.

'Yeah poor old Chelsea,' he said and finished the drink.

'What about the old Jags though? Even worse than Fulham.'

'What's that?'

'The Thistle man, the old Partick Thistle were relegated last season.'

'Ah. Scotch team eh?' he asked. 'Don't pay much heed.'

'Yeah you're right. Not much good up there,' said Charles.

'Bloody Celtic and Rangers,' the old fellow shook his head in disgust. 'Get them in here sometimes and the bloody Irish. Mostly go up the Angel they do. Bloody trouble they cause eh?'

'Give me another of those Dimples will you?'

'Yeah,' he smiled awkwardly. 'Like them do you? Can't say I do. Drop of gin now and then, yeah that's about it.'

Charles returned to his chair with his fresh drinks and sat quietly for about five minutes. Then he looked up at the bar.

'Hoy!' he shouted.

The deaf barman had regained his former position beneath the television set. He gave no indication of having heard.

'Hoy!' bawled Charles.

The old fellow jumped and turned angrily.

'What's up then? What's this Hoy all the time eh?'

'Well you're a bit deaf aren't you?'

'No need to bloody scream like that.'

'All right. I'm going out for a paper. Keep your eye on my drinks will you?' Charles got to his feet.

The barman muttered under his breath and began polishing some glasses.

Charles had to visit three newsagents before obtaining a copy of the *Sporting Life*. Nothing else could possibly do with all that back money lying about.

When he returned to the pub he noticed another customer sitting at a table opposite him in a corner. She was around ninety years old.

'Morning,' said Charles. 'Good morning missus.'

The old lady sucked her gums and smiled across at him, then looked up at the barman.

'Goshtorafokelch,' she said.

The barman looked from her to Charles before replying.

'Yeah I'll say eh?'

Bejasus thank God I've a paper to read. Perhaps this is an old folk's home in disguise.

'Hoy what time is it?' asked Charles when he had finished his drink.

The old fellow thought for a moment before answering.

'Well. Must be after twelve I reckon eh?'

'Think I'll be going then,' said Charles.

'You please yourself,' he muttered. 'Going to another shop then are you eh?'

'No it's not that man, I've got to go home, get a bath and that,' replied Charles. God love us why should I feel guilty about it? It's not as if he welcomed me with open arms.

'Will you be back then?' asked the old fellow.

'Well not today. Maybe tonight though, but if not definitely be back sometime.'

'Ah they all say that. Who cares eh?' he poured himself a gin. 'Fancy another short son?'

'What?' screeched Charles.

'Another short. Want a Dimple?'

'Why eh,' he looked over to the ancient lady for support. 'Why I'd really like another. Yeah thanks.'

'Bloody bottle's been here for years,' he poured a liberal glassful. 'Glad to get rid of the stuff.'

He passed the drink to Charles and watched him drink some.

'You really like it then eh?' he asked.

'It's a nice whisky. Yeah I quite like it.'

The barman opened a bottle of Guinness.

'Give that to her,' he said pointing to the old woman in the corner.

'Okay,' Charles carried it over. 'Here you are missus, the landlord sent it over for you.'

The old woman looked up and nodded her head with a smile.

'Patsorpooter,' she said.

'Yeah,' replied Charles smiling, 'yeah!'

He returned to the bar and downed his remaining whisky.

'Well I'll be off then and I'll be in again don't worry about that.'

'Hum,' muttered the barman polishing the counter. 'Yeah we'll see eh?' He moved away to the other side of the bar.

'Listen I'll be back,' cried Charles.

The old man was polishing glasses again and could not hear for the noise of the cloth rag.

'I'll see you later,' shouted Charles hopelessly.

He collected his newspaper and cigarettes from the table and made for the door. Christ this is really terrible. Can't understand what it's all about. Perhaps! No. I haven't a clue. Sooner I'm out of here the better. He stopped by the old lady with his hand on the door.

'Cheerio missus I'll be in next week sometime. Okay?'

She wiped a speck of foam from the tip of her nose.

'Deaf!' She cried, 'Deaf' and burst into laughter.

Charles had a quick look around but the aged barman had disappeared. He left quickly.

# The Best Man Advises

John returned with the drinks and carefully placed them on the table. 'Stop drinking the hard stuff?' He pushed a pint of heavy beer across.

'More or less,' Mick paused. 'Like a half now and then, if somebody else's doing the buying.' He shrugged and held up his right hand, thumb between the first two fingers. 'Got me like that man!'

'Bad as that?'

'Just about.' He frowned. 'Matter of fact I prefer her to hold the money. I'd do it in before Saturday mornings, on my own.' He smiled. 'Anyway you're worse than me so stop smirking.'

'Not me man,' he sat back comfortably. 'Well under control. Finished with it! No I mean it man, don't laugh. I'm telling you. Occasional game of cards and that's that.'

'Well good luck if it's true.'

'You're better drinking it, I suppose.'

'Yeah.' Mick stared thoughtfully at his glass.

'What's the forehead creasing for? Not agree?'

'Well I mean all the same really man. Piss it up against a wall or get beat in a photo! Same difference.'

'At least you get a drink for it!'

'Get a thrill if you gamble it.' He changed the subject. 'Anyway so you're still getting married?'

'Aye – even fixed up the honeymoon.'

'Where?'

'Not telling you, you bastard!'

Mick laughed aloud. 'Bet you it's Rothesay.'

'Rothesay my knickers!'

'Well why don't you tell me?'

'Bad luck! She says it's bad luck.'

'Jesus Christ I'm the best man.'

'Ach she's a bit superstitious Mick – tea leaves and that.'

'Once they go to those games man you've got to watch it. Be holding spiritual parties behind your back whenever you're out for a pint.'

'Fuck off.'

'Telling you man that's the way it gets them.'

'Her maw's a bit of a seance.'

'What?'

'A medium I mean, her maw – bit of a medium.'

'What? Christ!'

'Ach she's okay Mick, apart from that sort of stuff she's not a bad woman. Likes me too I think.'

'Ah well, more than that old bag of Betty's, Christ you want to see her? Or you don't want to see her! I never see her – dive out to the boozer whenever she shows up.'

'Posh isn't she?'

'Yeah from Bearsden. Thinks I abducted her daughter.' Mick shook his head. 'No wonder her man dropped dead.'

'Export?' asked John, rising with his empty glass. Mick nodded. He returned with two whiskies along with the beer.

'Halfs! Can you afford it?'

'Aye! Loaded!' John sat down. 'I've got a few quid. For the reception and the stag night and that.' He raised the whisky glass to make a toast. 'Well probably the last drink I'll have with you as a single man.'

'Aye. Good luck!' They drank about half the whisky; then Mick winked. 'Fancy getting blotto man? I mean really steamboats, fancy?'

'Suits me,' John grinned. 'What about you though?'

'I'm okay!' he shrugged. 'Got about four quid. Plenty!'

'Don't mean that.'

'What do you mean? Betty? You're jesting! She accepted all that years ago. Happy to see me bevied once in a while – makes her feel safe.'

'Well then Michael, long time since we got drunk together.'

'Probably the last . . .'

'Don't be so optimistic. Jesus Christ!'

'Well, I thought you'd have more sense John, I really did. I mean you could've taken me as an example.' He downed the remaining whisky and held up the empty tumbler. 'First half for three months!'

John smiled. 'Yeah, suppose I'll have to quiet down to a certain extent – screw the head with the money and that.' He paused. 'Betty looks after your money, I know that but you'd only punt it anyway so it's in your favour.'

'I know,' agreed Mick. 'I don't have any grumbles about finance. No, not at all. Freedom! I mean whenever you get bored you're off – London or someplace – that'll have to stop. You like to buy clothes – that'll have to stop.'

'Yeah,' he nodded. 'I know all that's got to stop to a certain extent . . .'

'Certain extent!' echoed Mick. 'What's this certain extent? Listen man I haven't bought a pair of socks for six months . . .'

'You always were a smelly bastard.'

'I'm dead serious John. Look . . .' he fingered the lapels of his jacket, '. . . I bought this eighteen months ago – only one I've got apart from that glen-checked effort with the fifteen-inch bottoms. Can't even pawn it man it's pathetic.' He stared mournfully into his empty whisky glass.

'Surely it's not that bad?'

'Whit!' shrieked Mick, causing several heads to look around.

They burst out laughing. Mick had to loosen his tie and open the top button of his shirt. 'Anyway,' he continued, 'same again?'

'Now what about the stag night?' John said when his companion returned.

'Honestly man can't make it. Would if I could.'

'Okay then it's finished.'

They remained drinking and reminiscing until the first bell rang at 9.50 p.m.

John said, 'Listen Mick what you fancy doing now, I mean . . .' he shrugged, '. . . we're not really steamboats are we?'

'No, you want to go for a meal or something?'

'Well let's get a carry-out first.'

'Aye!'

'I'll get it and we can settle after,' John said.

They travelled by taxi to John's single end in Maryhill. Immediately on entering Mick collected the key and went out again to the communal stairhead lavatory. When he returned a bottle of malt whisky and six cans of Export lay neatly on the table.

'Jesus Christ!'

'Drink we want – not an appetizer!' said John, searching in the cabinet for suitable cups.

'Okay!' cried Mick, taking two tumblers from his inside pocket and one half-pint glass from each side pocket. 'My contribution!' he said, smiling proudly.

'Silly bastard, you'll get caught one of these days.'

'No chance man – used to call me Fingers Henderson at school. Not remember?'

'How should I remember? You're years older than me.'

'Ah don't give me that patter. You joined the Scouts long before me.'

'You're a liar man, you got tossed out before I left the Cubs.'

Mick smiled and sank into an armchair.

'Pour us a drink,' he said. 'Can't be bothered arguing with you.'

'Cause you're wrong.'

'Up your arse.'

'Ah well never mind.' John handed him a whisky, and a beer.

'Good luck son you have my sympathy.' Mick gulped two-thirds of the whisky down. Then went on, 'Listen why don't you get off your mark. Get the first train to London in the morning before you start seeing ghosts with her and her mother? Cause I'm telling you man that's what'll happen.'

'You really talk some piss at times.'

'You don't believe me?'

John did not reply. He leaned across and topped up his guest's whisky.

'If I had your chance,' continued Mick, 'I'd be off in a flash – bags packed and offski.'

'Have I got to listen to this.' He groaned staring at the ceiling, then said, 'Anyway you could still do it for God sake. Why don't you instead of telling me?'

'Well the kid . . .'

'Ach you're always telling me he's up at your mother-in-law's with Betty all the time!'

'Yeah,' he said thoughtfully, 'You know something? I've thought about it a few times – but taking them with me, not just myself. Get away from old greeting face,' he paused, 'and Betty'll end up the same way if she carries on the way she's going.'

'How d'you mean?'

'Oh cause I can't get a job and that,' he lit a cigarette. 'Every time I see the old bag she's on at me about it. Really gets on my nerves, and Betty as well. I know she's thinking the same thing nowadays. In fact I was up with them a month ago, at

Bearsden and her maw started on. I sat watching the box not saying a word then Betty says there's a lot of truth in what she's saying. Jesus Christ!' Mick laughed loudly. 'I grabbed a nicker out her purse and went down the Black Bull, met a guy I knew and ended up at a party. Didn't go home until the next morning.'

'What happened?'

'Her and the kid were still at Bearsden. Stayed the night, maw told her I was probably gone for good and good riddance. One miserable nicker! Not even enough for a taxi to Central Station! Jesus Christ.' He looked so disgusted John could not help laughing. 'All right for you with a job and that – not seen a fiver for months. Had four quid tonight. Most I've had since I've been on the broo!'

'How'd you get it?'

'Birthday! Aye!' he laughed. 'Betty's maw – would you believe it? Gave her three quid for me, told her to buy me something cause I'd only fritter it away.'

'After what you've been saying about her too.'

'Ach she's loaded. Should see her house man, like Elder's Furniture Shop inside. Three quid! Gives her milk boy a bigger tip at Christmas. She really hates me.'

'Why d'you see her then?'

'Don't know. Suppose if I had a job I wouldn't go but she's not bad in ways – buys the kid stuff and drops Betty now and then. Extra couple of quid comes in handy.'

'Wouldn't be me.'

'What you talking about?' Mick sneered. 'Pride or some-thing?'

'For a couple of quid,' replied John quietly. 'I wouldn't take it.'

'Try living on a tenner a week then come and tell me!'

'Why don't you go south? Said you were thinking about it.'

'Well why should I man, I mean I'm from Glasgow. Why the hell should I go down there to live?'

'Work! I mean you liked it down there before you got married.'

'Well five years married! I've changed. It's not too bad, me and Betty get on okay together apart from her mother. Anyway . . .' he grinned, '. . . I like it on the broo. Plenty of time to read and that, it's not a bad life.'

'Never have a penny.'

'Don't need it. Hardly bothers me at all now. Really!'

'You're a liar.'

Mick laughed. 'I'm telling you man. Don't need any. Take a pound a week to myself and Betty buys me the tobacco. Tell me what I need money for?'

'That's no way to live.'

'Suits me.'

'What about the kid?'

'What about him?'

'Surely you want him to get something better?'

'Well if he wants to get a job down south I won't stop him.'

'Christ that's no way to live.'

Mick laughed again and refilled the glasses. 'Probably one of the most contented men in Britain when I think about it. If I could get an old cottage in the country – stay the summer – Glasgow in the winter. They send you your broo money when you stay in the wilds! Christ what a life eh?'

'So you've given up? Very surprised. Really am, I mean it's a load of piss. Balderdash!'

'What you going to do?' asked Mick still smiling.

'Don't know but I'm not going to give up like that.'

'Still going to night school?'

'Aye!'

'How's it coming on?'

'Not bad, thinking of going to college. Get enough highers for the uni. Strathclyde or something . . . Technical maybe. Engineering . . .'

'You?' Mick gaped in astonishment.

'Not think I've got the ability or something? Fuck me what's up at all? I'm only twenty-four for God sake!'

'Didn't mean that. Just can't imagine you,' he stopped and smilingly said, 'No offence.'

'Cheeky bastard! Seriously, you should try it too. All those books you read – no trouble, start putting them to use! If I can do it you'd guy in. How far!'

'Interesting maybe – but I'd still have to get a job after wouldn't I?'

John shook his head slowly.

'What you shaking your head about?'

'Doesn't matter.'

'I know it doesn't matter. You don't.'

'You'll have to get a job sooner or later.'

'Why?'

'Ach forget it man. Forget it.' He smiled. 'Just don't come tapping me when I hit the big time.'

Mick hooted derisively. They continued drinking silently for a time.

'Seriously though you've got no plans?'

'None at all,' answered Mick happily refilling the glasses once more.

'Must be something?'

'Might go into politics.'

'What?'

'Aye, there's this bird from the Young Socialists keeps coming up to see me and when she first saw my books asked me to join them. Says I'm a Natural Leader.'

'Young Socialists by fuck you're nearly thirty.'

'Don't know where you get these ideas about my age.'

'Come on.'

'No! Really! I'm only twenty-five! Anyway she keeps on

coming back. Suppose she must fancy me. Or maybe it's my mind she's after. Wants to save me – says I've given up too.' He grinned. 'Funnily enough she wants me to get my highers and all that piss. Nobody believes I'm really enjoying life. Fuck them all!' Mick declared with a flourish, knocking over his latest whisky in the process.

'You're blotto!'

'Shite!'

'Anyway . . .' John stood up and walked to the door.

'Want to see a doctor about your bladder.'

John laughed and staggered out to the lavatory. When he returned Mick was refilling the glasses again.

'Here's to your seance-in-law!' he cried and downed half his whisky.

'I'm steaming man you know that?' John sank into his chair and wearily lifted his glass. 'Went for that piss there . . . fresh air and that . . .'

'You know I might . . .' Mick broke off. 'When you getting married again?'

'Week on Saturday. Isn't it?'

'Week on Saturday eh?'

'I have this feeling I'm going to spew my guts.'

'Your house.'

'You staying the night?'

'No got to get back. Going to Bearsden the morning. Didn't tell you that eh? Jesus Christ! Sad! Going to Bearsden the morning. better go I think.'

'We'll finish the bottle before I'm sick. Should I be sick first? Who can tell eh?'

'Who can tell? Imagine going to Bearsden in the morning?'

'Not change your mind about the stag?'

'No. Like to – but reasons. Reasons!'

'Well you should be there. Best man and that should be at

the stag's what I think. Still as long as you get me to that church eh? Who cares?'

'Not me man. Couldn't care less. I'm going to see you week on Saturday bright and early if not before. No bother.'

'Repeat that?'

'Quite simple.' Mick stood up and stretched, almost toppling over with the effort.

'Here!' John poured another drink. 'For the road. Courage for Bearsden. Jesus!' He stared at the bottle. 'Almost done the lot in!'

'Oh!' John yelled and crashed down onto his armchair.

'What's up?'

'The robbery!'

'What?'

'Forgot to tell you the plan. Listen I'm going to rob banks in future. Natural Leader eh? Well listen to this – came to me last night in bed. A genius! Going to organise all the men on the broo. Guess how?'

'How?'

'Going to get a meeting together and put across the plan. Maybe two hundred guys on the broo right? Well imagine two hundred men walking into a bank. Okay give us the money! Christ a small army! Who could stop us? Nobody would know punters or robbers! Busies couldn't do fuck all either! Two hundred handed! What busies could stop us?'

'Jesus!'

'Brilliant eh?'

'Don't know if it'd work. You think it'd work?'

'Easy! No bother man. Two hundred handed! If they were all organised! Easy, and when we got outside we just split up and walk away and who could tell who was who? Nobody would recognise a face or anything. Genius! Anyway ponder on it. I'm going home. See you on the Saturday. Busies couldn't do a thing. Maybe do three or four a week. Wouldn't know what hit them. Ponder on it.'

'Okay.'

'You still going to be sick?'

'Probably.'

'Come on the broo! Sa great life. You can rob banks or anything. Screw Young Socialists. Fight with seance-in-laws. Can't beat it man.'

'Good night Natural Leader.'

'Still going to college and getting married and all that?'

'Without fail it's what's going to happen I think.'

'Headbanger! Remember and buy me a best man present.'

The door banged shut behind the best man, shortly before John retched the night up.

# Circumstances

They stopped outside the hospital gates. He could see the night porter peering through the window trying to identify the girl. The rain pattered relentlessly, although gently, down on the umbrella.

'I better go in,' the girl said with a half smile, staring in at the little office.

'Thought you were allowed till twelve before they closed the gates?' he asked.

She shrugged without replying and shuffling her feet began humming to herself.

'Anyway let's walk up the road a bit where there are no spies.'

'Oh Danny doesn't bother.' She stepped backwards into the shadows, expecting him to follow.

He saw the night porter turn the page of a newspaper with his left hand; he held a tea cup against his cheek with the other. Perhaps she was right. He didn't appear the least bit interested.

'Jilly, fancy a coffee?'

'In your flat I suppose?' she smiled, but not forlornly.

'Well it's only a room. But it's warm and I've got a chair.'

'That's not what I mean!'

He turned his coat collar up before replying.

'Listen, if you know any cafes still open we'll go there.'

He could not be bothered. What he did want to say was listen why don't you go in or why don't you come I'm getting tired and really what's the diff anyway? But she always had to play these little games all the time.

'I'm only kidding, Stuart,' she answered quickly, recognising that tone.

'Yeah!' He smiled. 'Sorry, Jilly. Come on, let's go and drink coffee. I'm too tired to rape you anyway.'

'Very funny!' she laughed.

Stuart had met her at the hospital dance four weeks ago and this was the sixth time they had gone out together. Cinema twice. Pub thrice. This evening Jilly had not finished until after eight, so they had dined in an Indian restaurant, had a few drinks and strolled about. When the rain started they made their way back to the hospital where she lived in. He did not find her tremendously attractive but she appeared to quite like him. They had never had sex together although at the beginning he had tried to persuade her at every opportunity. But now, she noticed his attempts becoming less frequent as were his jokes and funny remarks on the subject. She was half a head shorter than him, dressed quite well if six months behind in style, had short black hair and wore this brown corduroy coat he liked the first time he had seen it; but not the fifth. She had a sharp wee upturned nose. Nineteen years old, kissed with sealed lips and came from Bristol.

'No females allowed in here you know!' said Stuart, quietly turning the key in the lock. 'Under any circumstances!'

Jilly giggled looking up and down the street.

'I can only stay ten minutes,' she whispered, peering into the dark, musty-smelling hallway.

He beckoned her to follow and she crept upstairs without glancing back. This was a respectable bachelor-only house wholly maintained by an eighty-eight year old Italian landlady who preferred elderly, retired if possible, gentlemen. She had allowed Stuart in through her husband, who drank in his local, putting a word in. 'Steady boy,' he had told her. It was a clean, quiet house and during the six months he had stayed there he had only twice set eyes on another tenant. There was one other occasion when, shortly after closing time, a person had bumped against his door then fallen upstairs. When he investigated whoever it was had disappeared. He had concluded that the person lived directly above but could not be sure. He paid £3.50 per week for one medium-sized room containing a mighty bed which somewhat resembled his idea of the way an orthopaedic bed would look. It was shaped like a small but steep hill; four feet high at the top and half that high at the bottom. Occasionally he would awaken with his feet sticking out over the end and his head eighteen inches below the flat pillow. An unusual continental quilt covered the bed. The mattress interior seemed to be stuffed with empty potato crisp packets and startling crinkling sounds escaped whenever he turned over. It was extremely comfortable! He had no running water but there was an old marble-topped washing table and an enormous jug and basin. Underneath the table stood an enamel bucket and all three vessels plus the electric kettle were filled daily with fresh water by the landlady. There were neither gas nor electric cooking appliances. Under no circumstances was he allowed to cook even if he did supply his own stove; but he seldom ate out, preferring to buy in cold meat or cheese. Recently he had discovered tinned frankfurters which he emptied into the kettle with one or two eggs. When the water boiled for three minutes, both the sausages and the eggs would be ready to be eaten. Only snag was, apart from the spout being very narrow, that the hole in the kettle was barely 3" in diameter and this meant having to spear each frankfurter out individually, by fork, which required skill; and occasionally an egg would crack when lowered by spoon and dropped onto the kettle bottom, causing the water to become cobwebby from the escaping egg white. Fortunately the coffee flavour always seemed unimpaired. He was secretly proud of his ingenuity but could not display it to Jilly as he had neither egg nor frankfurter. Still she did accept the chair, and the coffee. He switched on the gas fire.

'Very quiet house,' she said presently.

'Haunted.'

Jilly smiled her disbelief.

'You don't believe me? There's things go bump in the night here!'

'I don't believe you. No.'

'Okay.' Sitting facing her on the carpet he began twiddling the knobs of his transistor radio. 'What's Luxembourg again?' he asked.

'208 meters. If I believed everything you told me I'd go mad or something.'

'Doesn't bother me if you don't want to hear about it.' He paused. 'I'm going to tell you anyway.' He switched off the radio and continued in a low growling kind of stage voice. 'One dark black winter's evening just after closing time, around the turn of the century, an aged retired navvy was returning from the boozer . . .'

'Retired what?'

'Navvy, and he was still wearing his Wellingtons – was returning from the boozer quietly singing this shanty to himself when he opened the front door and climbed the stairs,' Stuart paused, pointing to his door, 'just as he passed this very door to go up to his room he stopped and there at the top of the stairs he saw this death's head staring at him. Well he staggered back letting out this bloodcurdling scream and toppled downstairs banging into this door on the way to his doom.'

'Did he?' asked the girl politely.

'Yeah really! They say to this day if you climb the stairs occasionally just after closing time you can sometimes see a death's head wearing a pair of Wellington boots. I know it's hard to believe but there it is.'

Jilly stared far above his head.

'Too much bloody interference at this time of night,' said Stuart back with the transistor. 'You want Radio One?'

'I don't mind,' she sang during a chorus.

Why the hell didn't she go? Sitting there like Raquel Welch! Anyway if she did fancy him surely she'd want to kip up with him – at least for the night, Good God! Still he didn't have to get up for work so who cared? But if she stayed out too late they'd lock her out and not open up without a steward's inquiry. Get chucked out the house if Arrivederci Roma found her – or traces.

'Want another cup of coffee?'

'I don't mind.'

'Well yes or no?'

'If you're having one.'

'I'm not having one but if you want one well just go ahead and say so eh?'

'I'm not fussy.'

Jesus why didn't she get up and go?

'Plenty of books there if you want a read . . . ?' he gestured vaguely towards the side of the bed where a pile of paperbacks lay.

'No thanks I'm not much of a reader.'

He poked a strip of newspaper through the grill of the gas fire and lit a cigarette.

'Did you never smoke?'

'Yes, quite heavily, but I gave it up last year.'

'Good for you. I wish . . .' He lacked the energy to finish the sentence.

'There's jobs going in the hospital for porters and storemen.'

'Are there?'

'Yes and they earn a good wage. The man you see is a Mr Harvey. They're desperate for staff.'

Perhaps she only went out with him in an attempt to recruit him for the position of porter. Maybe she worked in Personnel. Office she had said.

'What song's that again? It's nice.'

'Ten Guitars. I've always liked that one,' she replied. 'It was only a B-side.'

'Like the fast ones myself.'

'You would!'

'Eh?'

What was this? Note of encouragement? Hint perhaps, after all this time? What the hell was he supposed to do? Had no desire to play around tonight without going the whole road. Very bad on the nerves that. Anyway she didn't have the brains to drop hints. Didn't even have the brains to . . .

'What was that?' cried the girl.

'What?'

'That noise,' she looked at the door.

'Ssh, quietly,' he whispered. 'Might be the old one creeping about. Or maybe someone going to the lav. Don't want her to find out.'

'Oh!' she replied, relieved.

'You didn't believe that death's head twaddle did you?'

'Of course not, I'm used to you by now!'

What did she mean by that? He stood up and walked past her to the cupboard, lifted the alarm clock down and wound it. After setting it back he stared at her shoulders as she gazed at the gas fire while humming to herself. Well had to do something; this was getting ridiculous. He stepped over to the chair and kissed the nape of her neck. She did not move. He unbuttoned her blouse down the back. She allowed it to slide off her shoulders and lie behind her on the chair; then she retrieved it and folding it, placed it neatly by the bed. Meanwhile he fumbled with the hooks on her bra.

'What d'you think you're playing at?' she asked.

'Taking off your clothes, but I'm stuck.' Then he discovered the catch.

'No, I'm not,' he added.

'Well I hope you're enjoying yourself.'

But he had been this far before; once in the alley behind the hospital he had almost succeeded in taking her pants down! He let the bra remain hanging from her shoulders. Moving around to face her, he took both her hands and pulled her to her feet and kissed her. Still unsure but almost allowing himself to believe this was it, he hesitated. Jilly unzipped her skirt and stepping out from it crawled onto the bed and under the quilt. She unconcernedly stretched over and strung her bra over the chair.

'Never seen one of these before,' she said unaware of his incredulous stare.

'Sa continental quilt!' he answered at last.

Still rather dazed, he undressed down to his socks and pants, and walked across to switch off the light. She giggled.

'What's up?'

'You in your socks and thin legs.' She laughed again rather shrilly.

'Lucky I'm not wearing Wellington boots!' He grinned nervously, shrugged and marched forward.

Stuart had forgotten to change the set time of the clock and so it alarmed at ten o'clock as usual. Recognising the severity of the situation he jumped out of bed immediately and dressed rapidly. The landlady rose at dawn and would be well away cleaning by this time. Fortunately she would not come in: when he left the house in the morning he would leave the door open and she knew it was then safe to enter but if the door was closed she waited. He told Jilly to hurry. He could imagine the confrontation if the old one were to enter unannounced.

'Come on Jilly,' he urged.

She found her pants amongst the fankled sheets at the foot of the bed and quickly slipped them on. Attempting to pull on her tights she toppled onto the bed and giggled.

'Ssh for God sake,' he whispered. 'The old one's got ears like an elephant.'

Finally she was ready and he went out closing the door behind him. He looked upstairs and downstairs but no sign of her. Had to be out shopping! He was now standing in the hallway.

'Quick!' he roared up the two flights of stairs.

It made no difference how much noise they made now. He was not in the least worried about the other tenants. Perhaps there were no other tenants! Then the girl came clattering downstairs clutching her coat and bag.

'Got everything?' he asked.

She nodded unable to speak.

He opened the front door quietly and peered up the street. No one! Grabbing her by the hand he tugged her down the seven steps to the pavement. They strode down the street in the opposite direction to which the old woman always returned.

Shortly after midday he came back to the house. They had eaten breakfast then Jilly had gone into work, against his wishes. They had arranged to meet outside the hospital gates at 5.30 that evening.

He walked upstairs and into his room almost tripping over the suitcase.

'Your goods all in there!' said the landlady, suddenly materializing on the landing behind him.

'What?'

'I'm not silly!' cried the old woman. 'You had woman in my house last night. I pack in all your goods.'

'No I didn't! A woman!'

'Come on don't tell me. I know! I'm not silly!' She advanced towards him.

'Not me!' he protested, backing away.

'I tell Mr Pernacci no! No young man! But no, he say you're nice boy. Steady!' Her angular nose wrinkled in disgust. 'This the way you treat us eh?' she yelled.

Stuart could only shrug – after all she was eighty-eight.

'And Mr Clark say he hear noises through the night.'

'Did he?' He could not restrain the broad grin appearing.

'Aah now you laugh eh. Come on. On you go out. Out!'

'Okay,' he lifted the suitcase, 'but I should get a rent rebate.'

'Aah please. Not be cheeky with me.'

'I'm not being cheeky. But it's not very nice throwing someone out into the street like this, is it?'

He walked downstairs with the old lady following, clutching her skirts.

'Don't talk. Not very nice with woman in my house. Never before in many many years.' She paused. 'Think of your mother! No I think you never do that.'

'I'm a young man Mrs Pernacci you must expect it.' He opened the door. 'You won't reconsider?'

'No. Come on. Out you go. Can't behave like this in people's houses.'

Stuart sadly shook his head.

'You must mend yourself,' continued the landlady. 'Now please go, Mr Pernacci be very angry with you.'

'No he won't!'

'Yes yes, he will be.' Her old eyes widened. 'Now cheerio please.'

'Cheerio!' he called as the door slammed shut.

The rain fell steadily as he lugged the suitcase around the corner to his local. Jilly was surprised to see him carrying it when they met that evening.

# New Business

Dougie stood up and said that it was time to go. Willie nodded and finished his beer before leaving. The union meetings were held in a small office, part of the district town hall, and although timed to begin at 7.30 prompt, seldom started before eight o'clock. They arrived at 8.10 to find the room deserted. A passing janitor informed them that someone had poked his head round about ten minutes ago and suggested that they take a seat and have a smoke if they wanted. Dougie laughed.

'Told you,' he said.

'Well it was a warm day man and you can't really blame them. We did have a couple ourselves.'

Dougie stared at him for a moment.

'You're off your head anyway,' he said. 'I mean you don't really think they'll discuss the Bill do you?'

'We'll see.'

The sounds of approaching voices accompanied by loud laughter were preceded into the room by an old man who walked slowly down the passageway and sat on a chair in the corner, in the second front row. Then the door opened and in came the Chairman and the Shop Steward of the branch, followed by assorted members of the committee and around a dozen ordinary union members. The committee men strode to the far end of the room and sat down behind the long table where the Shop Steward proceeded to lay out some sheets of paper and his tobacco tin. The ordinary members, now seated on the chairs on the other side of the table, were speaking amongst themselves. Dougie was discussing the day's racing with the fellow in front when the Chairman called the meeting to order and apologised for the absence of the Secretary. Someone at the back loudly whispered something about Ibrox Park and the Chairman quickly retorted that he wasn't far wrong there and laughed with the rest.

'Anyway,' he continued, 'our good friend and scrutineer Brother Reilly has kindly offered to stand in. So, Gus!'

Gus MacDonald the Shop Steward passed some papers across to Brother Reilly, and remarked aside to the Chairman:

'Couple of new faces tonight eh!' He continued loudly, 'Well Brothers if Brother Reilly reads us last month's Minutes we'll get it started eh?'

'Aye well . . .' began the Acting Secretary, adjusting his spectacles before beginning.


'And so if there's no objections I'll sign for a True Record,' said the Chairman when the Acting Secretary had read the last Minute.

'Don't see any,' said Reilly, peering around the room.

'Any Matters Arising?' asked the Chairman as he signed.

'What about this canteen business eh?' cried a fellow sitting near the front.

'No!' replied the Chairman.

'Not a Matter Arising,' said the Acting Secretary.

'What's going to get done?' continued the fellow.

The Chairman glanced across at the Shop Steward before answering. 'Later Tam.' He leaned over and whispered something to the Acting Secretary.

But the fellow persisted. 'Well I hope so because . . .'

'Tam!' cried Brother Reilly, shaking his head in exasperation.

'Okay,' interrupted the Shop Steward, darting a look at the

Chairman. 'I got on to the manager about that Tam and he said there's nothing he can do. Said it was Head Office's decision and he'd take it to them, but as I told you last month they're only allowed to put on two dinners and all Head Office'll say is there's no demand.'

'No demand!' echoed Tam, amazed. 'No demand! Christ there's plenty! Plenty uses the bloody place; and we never get a choice. Bloody terrible!'

'Aye I know Tam.' The Shop Steward gestured vaguely about the table.

'You know? Christ every day of the week stew or mince. Bloody stew or mince all the time Gus! Bloody ridiculous! Surely they can give us a better choice than that?'

'Well that's what I told the manager and he . . .'

'Aye you're right Tam, it's a disgrace,' called another man.

'Aye and you'd be cheaper eating in a bloody restaurant,' cried someone in the front row.

'Aye you're right there!' agreed another.

'Order!' demanded the Chairman. 'A minute! One at a time eh?'

'Well the manager . . .' began the Shop Steward.

'Fuck the manager – bloody mince – every day of the week since . . .'

'Bar Friday Tam, eh?' cried a voice from the back.

'Aye a bit of scabby fish. Bloody out of order.' Tam sat back, arms folded and shoulders erect.

'Well . . .' tried Brother MacDonald.

'Christ!' Tam looked somewhere over the heads of the committee.

'Okay! Order!' called the Chairman. 'We've done all this last month, Brother Smith and Gus says the manager's getting on to Head Office about it so we'll just have to wait and see the score. Okay?'

Tam muttered something to his neighbour.

'Okay?' repeated the Chairman.

Tam shrugged.

'Right,' continued the Chairman. 'Anything else?'

'Aye Brother,' grunted the old man who sat in the corner in the second front row. 'What about the paper?'

'Yes,' replied the Chairman, amid laughter, 'Correspondence Sammy, Correspondence.'

'In a minute Sammy, okay?' said the Shop Steward.

'Aye well.' The old timer rocked back and forth, nodding to himself.

'Right then Brothers if that's the lot . . .' The Chairman looked around but on seeing no more queries, continued. 'Okay then. Brother MacDonald'll read us the Correspondence.'

'Well Brothers, not much tonight.' He withdrew a few envelopes from his briefcase and began reading the contents aloud. No one interrupted this time. On opening the last letter he paused and glancing across at the old man, said with mock severity: 'Concerning toilet paper.'

A few amused looks and one or two quips greeted the reading of this letter. It confirmed that in future an adequate supply of toilet paper (soft) would be provided, subject to the Shop Steward's request on behalf of the branch members.

'Okay Sammy?' asked the Shop Steward.

'Aye Brother. They better!' added the old man darkly.


'People are always knocking his *Daily Record*,' whispered Dougie, 'and using it to wipe their arse.'

Willie smiled without replying.


'We had two delegates over to see our Brothers in Kilmarnock last week,' the Chairman cleared his throat, 'about their pay claim and . . . Brother Reilly!'

'Aye me and Boabbie went to see them at their meeting. They're looking for 15% and they'll get it Lindsay says. He thinks they should've went for twenty.'

'Hum,' muttered the Chairman, then whispered something to MacDonald.

'And that's it more or less. Oh Sammy, Brother Lindsay was asking for you. Said to tell you him and Etty would be through to see how you're doing.'

'Aye Brother.'

'How much we asking anyway?' called a man from the back.

'Fifteen Charlie,' answered Brother Reilly.

'That's New Business,' interjected the Chairman.

'What we're waiting for.' Dougie spoke out the corner of his mouth.

Willie nodded.

'Oh another thing,' Reilly went on, 'You want to see their facilities through there – snooker and table tennis and that. You want to see it! They run handicap competitions all the time and Lindsay says some of the staff goes in for them too.'

'Aye we've had a few talks on this subject before Brothers,' said the Chairman.

'Aye,' agreed the Shop Steward. 'Remember the last one?'

'Not likely to forget,' said some men, grinning in appreciation.

'Anyway if that's it Brother?'

'Aye, just thought I'd mention it,' replied the Acting Secretary.

'No harm done,' said the Chairman. 'Right Brothers. New Business.'

'The pay claim!' shouted Tam. 'What about asking for twenty?'

'No point Brother,' answered the Shop Steward. 'We've no chance of getting fifteen as it is.'

'If Kilmarnock gets it – we better!' remarked someone.

'We're already getting more than them. The management are just bringing them up to our level.'

'Our level?'

'Well,' grinned MacDonald, 'not quite Brother; but no too far away.'

'I move we put in for twenty!' declared Tam, rising to his feet.

'Jesus Christ!' muttered the Chairman.

'Tam there's no chance. Waste of bloody time!' cried the Shop Steward.

'Well fifteen . . .' Tam paused. 'We ask for twenty we'll definitely get fifteen.'

The Chairman struck a match and relit his long-dead pipe. He spoke quietly to the Acting Secretary, seemingly without any interest in the current discussion.

'Anybody second that motion?' asked the Shop Steward hopelessly, after a moment.

'Aye me!' said Tam's neighbour, rising and standing shoulder to elbow with his tall friend.

MacDonald hesitated.

'Brothers,' said the Chairman at last, 'this has been gone into very carefully. We are asking fifteen and that's that. Waste of time asking more. Let's wait and see what happens through at Kilmarnock first eh?'

A few of the members nodded their agreement.

'Think you should withdraw the motion,' stated the Chairman after a short pause.

'Aye,' agreed Tam's neighbour without hesitation.

Tam sat down shaking his head in disgust.

\* \* \*

'What about this business about the apprentice?' asked a man in the front row.

The Chairman turned to Brother Reilly who quickly explained the facts to him.

'It's out of order that one of the clerks has only to open his mouth and the boy's hauled up in front of the manager,' continued the man.

'Well he shouldn't have swore at him in the first place Brother,' said the Shop Steward.

'Ach it's out of order.'

'He shouldn't have been in their toilet in the first place,' said the Chairman.

'Christ he had the runs! What's he supposed to do?'

'That's right he couldn't wait,' said a voice from the back.

'He only got a warning . . .'

'I'll speak to the manager,' remarked the Shop Steward.

'Says they've got towels in there,' grumbled old Sammy.

'Anyway,' said the Chairman, 'that's it?'

'What about a games room or something, snooker or something?' asked Tam.

'Well!' called the Chairman.

'I move that we try again to get a snooker table,' affirmed Tam.

'I second that motion Brother,' said the Acting Secretary.

The Chairman looked at his watch before saying: 'Nothing else then?'

'I could do with a pint,' said the Shop Steward, shuffling his sheaves of foolscap paper as he rose to his feet.

'A minute!' cried Willie in a voice two octaves higher than usual.

Dougie rubbed his hands together and lowered himself further down in his seat.

'Well Brother?' called the Shop Steward. The Chairman was

knocking his pipe bowl out, against his shoe.

'About the Bill. The second reading takes place at the end of the week and if nothing worthwhile is done quickly it will be passed through without any opposition worth talking about.'

A murmur travelled through the room. The Shop Steward sat down heavily.

'What's he talking about?' asked someone.

'When did he start in the job?' asked another.

'Never get a pint now,' muttered Brother Reilly.

'You mean THE "Bill"?' queried the Chairman.

'Of course,' replied Willie. 'As far as I can ascertain there have been no individual points raised, neither has the "Bill" as a whole ever been discussed – at any of your branch meetings.'

Someone at the back laughed. Old Sammy shuffled up the passageway and out, quietly closing the door behind him.

'He's a student!' confirmed someone at the back.

'Well son,' explained the Shop Steward, 'naturally we don't like it but it has to get done. I mean it had to come.'

'What's it all about?' asked Tam.

'It means one cannot strike unofficially, for one thing,' said Willie.

'That right?' Tam said to the table.

'Well . . . aye,' answered the Shop Steward, 'but all it means is our strikes'll all be official from now on.' He rolled a cigarette.

'For example,' persisted Willie, 'if you were to decide to strike because the management refused to meet your demands for adequate toilet paper, and the union would neither support nor back your action, you could be jailed.'

'What!'

'What was that?'

'Okay son,' commented the Chairman. Turning to Tam he said, 'He's talking nonsense. The management are giving us the paper anyway.'

'I didn't know anything about it,' insisted Tam glaring around the room.

'It's on sale at the Post Office,' someone shouted from the back.

'But Brother what's this about the jail for striking?' asked an elderly man sitting in the front row.

'Nobody's getting the jail for striking!' cried the exasperated Chairman.

'Unless any of you take unofficial action,' added Willie.

'Right son that's it finished. They've taken this decision at Headquarters and that's it. It's *ultra vires!*'

'I am surprised the matter has not been discussed . . .'

'Okay kid it's finished,' said the Acting Secretary. 'It's just politics anyway.'

'So if there's nothing else Brothers . . . ?'

'I don't know the score here about all this,' said Tam.

'Get it at any Post Office; been on sale for weeks,' the Shop Steward said quickly as he closed his briefcase.

'Aye okay.' Tam hitched up his trousers then pointed a finger at him.

'You remember and see the manager about that bloody canteen.'

'Aye, don't worry about that Tam. I'll go and see the bastard first thing in the morning.'

'Right then.' He nodded down to his neighbour and they strode purposefully from the room.

'Be lucky to catch a pint,' they heard Tam's neighbour say.

'Right Brothers I think we'll wind it up here.' The Chairman stood up and the other committee members filed down the passageway after him.

'Should come for a drink with us son,' said the Chairman, pausing as he passed Willie's row. 'Eh Gus?'

'Aye son, we like a good argument,' said the Shop Steward.

'As long as it's no about religion,' affirmed the Chairman. 'OK then lads? See you tomorrow.'

When everyone had left the room Dougie turned to his companion and hooted derisively.

Willie scratched his head.

# This Morning

Sam pulled on his boots and laced them, then lay back in the old armchair. It was too early yet. The newspaper bundles would hardly have arrived so there was no point in leaving for a while. He stared up at his books which were arranged in alphabetical order on the wooden shelves he had built a couple of years ago. Nowadays he looked up at them more than he read them. Perhaps he would take a walk up the jumble sale on Saturday, see if there was anything doing.

He sighed deeply, aware of the phlegm rumble in his chest. He pulled himself up from the chair and filled the kettle. A hell of an amount of tea passed through him these days. He shook his head and opened the tobacco tin to roll a cigarette; then returned to his chair and tore a strip from yesterday's paper, and got a light from the fire. Choking on the first drag Sam spat out some shreds of tobacco onto the grate. He ran his tongue along the roof of his mouth. It tasted vaguely of whisky. He had had none for a month.

The kettle whistled and he jumped up from the armchair, and turned the gas off. He rinsed out the tea pot and hand-measured the tea into it before pouring in the boiling water. He placed the pot on the fire surround to infuse.

Would soon be a quarter to six and time to get going. Doing a paper round at his age? Why not? He had started two months ago and never regretted it. The customers were more embarrassed than he was, but slow to tip. One or two of the boys made over thirty bob a week in tips. Sam had yet to make more than a pound. Still it helped his wage up to about two and a half so why grumble. Five minutes to go.

Sam threw the tea dregs into the fire and watched the coal sizzle a moment. Used tea leaves burned well and smelled good. Perhaps he ought to write in to the papers about it; win a guinea or a prize or something. Over the crumpled jacket he put on the old Crombie coat he had found in a bazaar up Byres Road. It cost him four bob. Must have been given in error surely! Good God. He put on the corduroy bunnet.

He lived in a single end in Partick down near South Street and his close was the last remaining one still inhabited by paying tenants. The rest of the tenement building was being slowly demolished. Old Rachel still hid in number seventeen but nobody official knew that. She had moved in with the demolishers and so far had outstayed them. Her family had parked her away in an old folks' home where she had managed to stay for six weeks before leaving and dossing around Anderston. Sam had found her there three weeks later. They had known each other for a long long time and he reckoned she could give him twenty years; he had turned seventy, five months ago. She swore to having milked cows in MacGregor's farm at Partick Cross when she was a girl. Sam could not remember ever having heard of a farm at Partick Cross.

The snow lay thick on the ground, covering the heaps of rubble strewn around the waste ground. Still dark. Nearly three hours before the street lights were switched off.

Sam closed the door and set off up Purdon Street and along Dunbarton Road. He turned into the Kelvin Way making for Gibson Street where the newsagent he worked for had her shop. He arrived just as she opened.

'Morning Mrs Johnstone! How are you?' he asked.

'Freezing Samuel,' she smiled bravely. 'Put on the kettle and we'll have a quick cuppa.'

He helped her in with the bundles before going through to the back. When he returned with the tea Mrs Johnstone had almost completed the sorting.

'Think the weather's getting worse these days,' she said. Sam nodded as he rolled the cigarette. 'Makes you wonder what we pay the weather men for.'

'Aye!' he muttered and lit up.

'So dear for coal as well. It's awful!'

'Aye!' he paused, sipping the tea. 'Makes you appreciate the summer.'

'I suppose so. Do you ever go away?'

'Aye!' He peered at her over the cup. 'Went down to Ayr this year.'

'Oh Burns' country!' she smiled. 'I like Ayrshire. Culzean Castle's nice. Did you see it?'

'No!'

'Burns' Cottage?'

Sam grinned, 'I was racing.'

'Oh! Horses?' Her eyebrows arched.

'Aye!' He finished the tea. 'Think I'll be off now.'

'I've laid them out. Tobacco's there too.'

'Aye well,' he lifted the papers. 'See you in the morning then.'

'Aye if we're alive touch wood!' She thumped the counter.

'Aye well,' he clicked his teeth together. 'Cheerio!'


Sam delivered his last newspaper shortly before eight and then headed for home. The streets were busier now and the first office workers were already out and creeping about. The snow had stopped falling and lay deep and soft, muffling the traffic noise. His face seemed redder and his purple nose looked bluer than ever. His hands and feet tingled. Only the rumble from the depths of his belly caused him any discomfort. The thought of a hot meal quickened his step. Four or five days ago Rachel had brought him a large cauldron of soup. He had hardly touched anything else since then; and about a quarter still remained. It improved with age. He entered number seventeen and thrust a *Daily Record* through the letter box; a transistor blared out. Rachel woke up at 6.30 every morning out of habit, drank three or four pints of tea and switched on the radio before returning to bed. Said it helped her get back to sleep. Inside his own room he lit the stove under the soup. The good smell of the broth soon filled the room and by the time he had the fire going, it was ready. He filled the large bowl brimful of steaming broth and buttered two slices of bread and sat down. Rice and bits of bacon and all kinds of vegetables floated around. He dipped the bread in until it was so thoroughly saturated he had to tilt his head back when swallowing lest part fall off and down his neck. Then he finished and sank onto the armchair raising the soles of his feet in front of the now roaring fire. He rolled a thick cigarette and settled back occasionally sipping from the mug of tea. He hardly had enough energy to read the paper.

He awoke with a start and looked up at the clock on the mantle piece; after 10.30, time to be going. He rinsed his mouth out with the cold tea dregs then spat into the dying fire. He splashed the ice-cold tap water on his face and neck; and drying vigorously felt the stiffness leaving him. He undressed and changed clothing, on went the white shirt and dark red tie over which came the navy serge three-piece suit. He felt fine.

A dozen people queued behind him at the bus stop before Partick Cross subway station. The constant flow of traffic had almost cleared the snow completely but the gutter was overflowing with black slush and dirty water. Every time a vehicle passed in the inside lane the queue jumped back out of reach of the spray. One or two had been caught unawares and an extremely fat lady was now standing in slush-lined boots. Sam had been waiting thirty minutes and his feet were numb. The people spoke amongst themselves about the delay and the fat lady seemed to be chairing the discussion. She kept trying to involve him in his role as the head of the queue but Sam had plenty of experience in playing deaf. He could also feign senility quite easily. Eventually the bus came and he was the first of the five only allowed on to stand inside. What a racket! Ninety-eight per cent of the passengers were women and children clacking and yapping. He heard the slush-lined lady arguing with the conductor.

'An hour I waited . . .' she screeched, 'an hour!'

'You never waited an hour missus.'

'I did so.'

'No you never!'

'But I did, you just ask that old man there!' Sam could feel her podgy finger pointing somewhere between his shoulder blades. Good God! 'Go on, just you ask him!' she cried.

'Missus I don't have to ask anybody . . .' relief surged through Sam, '. . . I know for a fact you couldn't have waited any more than half an hour.' He paused. 'So shut up or I'll throw you off the fucking bus!'

Silence descended over the lower deck as the conductor retreated in a scarlet rage to the front of the bus where he resumed his eight-hour stance by the driver.

'Well!' cried the outraged slush looking around her.

'Is that not a disgrace?' came a hoarse whisper from the back.

The conductor wheeled and glared at the hastily averted eyes on either side of the passageway. 'Come on!' he said evenly. 'Come on speak up!' He turned back in disgust then climbed to the top deck.

'Well you think he'd be ashamed of himself!' said someone.

'Huh!' replied the slush. 'Not them. Only a public servant as well.'

'Yes you're right there,' agreed a skinny bespectacled lady wearing an enormous fur coat. 'And to think we pay their wages! I remember once . . .'

She turned completely around in her seat near the front before continuing, 'when this one . . .'

At this point Sam escaped upstairs as a passenger came down. The atmosphere in the upper deck was thick with cigarette and pipe smoke, and without one window open half of the travellers were sputtering and coughing their lungs onto the floor. Sam joined them; better inhaling his own smoke than someone else's. A whisky would be like nectar. Even another cup of tea would go down well.

Under the Central Station bridge Sam thankfully alighted and walked along to the Royal Billiard Saloon. A few labourers were out clearing snow and slush from the road. It was very cold.

He walked downstairs and through the swing doors of the hall. Although barely opened, half the thirty tables were in use. Striding across to the number-one table he stopped and, nodding to one or two of the spectators, stood by the marker.

'Morning Sam,' the latter said quietly.

'Aye Joe, how are things?'

'Not bad!' He indicated one of the players. 'Needs a ball!'

The man potted the brown, positioning himself well on the blue which he shot into the middle bag, the pink lay over a corner pocket.

'Okay Danny I believe you,' said his opponent. He smiled.

'Want a clear?' asked the winner.

'Aye a clear head!' laughed the man.

'Quite a good game though.'

'Aye.' He smiled slowly as he handed the two notes over. 'It's a hundred and thirty I should get. I'll see you.'

'Aye cheerio John.' Danny glanced around but found no response to the unspoken challenge. He noticed Sam for the first time. 'Sam! Where've you been?' He laughed. 'Want a game of billiards?'

'No.'

'Pint?'

'Now that's a better idea.'

'Thought you'd appreciate it.'

Inside the adjacent pub Danny ordered a pint of lager for himself and a half and a bottle of beer for Sam. He carried the drinks across to the table where Sam was sitting reading his *Sporting Life*. He looked up, and said: 'Not a bad card.'

'Yeah I may have a bet. Cheers!'

Sam nodded and sipped the whisky.

'First of the day's always the best,' Danny said, smacking his lips.

'First of the month more like.'

'What?'

'Aye that's how you haven't seen me for a while. Doctor's orders – I've been staying out the path of temptation.'

'What,' asked Danny, 'your liver?'

'Christ knows but he told me to leave off it all together for a bit, especially the whisky.'

'If I'd known I'd not got you one.'

'Ach I'd have bought one for myself. What's the point? Only prolong the agony.' He grinned.

'Thought you had a certainty picked out for the Lincoln?' laughed Danny.

'Oh I'll hang about till then, don't worry about that.' He drained the last drop of whisky into his beer.

'Fancy going down to Ayr tomorrow?'

'Probably be abandoned.'

'Aye,' agreed Danny. 'Fancy a pie and beans?' He rose from the table.

'No – not for me. Had some of old Rachel's soup at half past eight this morning.' He smiled. 'Two platefuls.'

'Jesus Christ!'

'Aye and if I can take that I can drink anything. Anything at all!' They both laughed and Sam gave his empty glasses to the younger man. He rolled a cigarette mechanically, deep in thought and unaware of the bar rapidly filling with workers on their lunch hour. 'Ach!' The grunt echoed hoarsely up from his boots.

'What's up?'

He had not noticed Danny returning. He shrugged. 'What age are you again?'

'Thirty!'

'Time you were married.' He sipped his beer.

'Kidding?'

'Had two kids at your age!'

'But that was the good old days.' Danny snorted and took a long swig of lager.

'Aye I don't blame you!' Sam grinned.

'Might go back to London.'

'Been back a while now.'

'Nearly a year,' he said swirling the beer around inside the glass, 'I miss it.'

'Aye this place is played out.'

'Hardly recognised it when I came back. See Anderston?'

'Jesus what a state.'

'Suppose it's progress Sam.'

'Progress my arse!'

Danny laughed. 'Why don't you go back south?'

'Ha ha ha,' said Sam.

'Why not?'

'Know how long I've been away? Over eight years! Fact, probably nearer ten apart from Goodwood once and that time we all went down for the Guineas.'

'Kashmir?'

'Aye, sevens I think it was.'

'That's right,' said Danny. 'Christ remember Jimmy Lindley storming up that hill. What a race!'

'We done well that meeting.'

'You caught Glad Rags and told nobody till afterwards.'

Sam laughed. 'Aye and Charlie won four and a half grand and wound up skint on Monday morning. Crazy!'

They lapsed into silence.

'Freddie was asking how you were doing,' said Danny after a time. 'Said to get in touch with him if you fancy going back.'

'Suppose I could get a few quid together by March . . .'

'To go down?'

'Ach who's kidding who?' He paused. 'I'd probably collapse in the train. Anyway what about old Rachel?'

'She could survive in the jungle.'

'Aye! Maybe . . .' He swallowed the whisky. 'What you doing over Christmas?'

'Don't know yet. Probably go to the sister's. How about you?'

'Ah,' he smiled. 'Old Rachel's trying to get me into the old folk's party.'

'Fancy it?'

'You must be joking – Christ they're even having a Santa Claus. Imagine it? He'll probably be the youngest person there.' They laughed loudly.

'Course you'll get some good grub there.'

'Aye if you sing a solo Christmas carol.' His face wrinkled in disgust. 'Worse than a Sally Ann skipper!'

'Another?'

'No I'm just going.'

Danny did not reply.

'Put a line on – three races on the box,' explained Sam.

'Aye okay man. You be in tomorrow?'

Sam got to his feet and swallowed the last of the beer before replying: 'Definitely!' He turned and walked to the door.

'Hey!' called Danny. Sam wheeled. 'Win a few quid for Ayr tomorrow eh?'

Sam laughed. He travelled home by subway.

# Nice to be Nice

Strange thing wis it stertit oan a Wedinsday, A mean nothin ever sterts oan a Wedinsday kis it's the day afore pay day in A'm ey skint. Mibby git a buckshee pint roon the Anchor, bit that's aboot it. Anywey it wis efter nine in A wis thinkin aboot gin hame kis A hidny a light whin Boab McCann threw is a dollir in A boat masel in auld Erchie a pint. The auld yin hid two boab ay his ain so A took it in won a couple a gemms a dominoes. Didny win much bit enough tay git is a hauf boattle a Lanny. Tae tell ye the truth A'm no fussy fir the wine bit auld Erchie'll guzzle it tae it comes oot his ears – A'm tellin ye! A'll drink it mine ye bit if A've goat a couple a quid A'd rethir git a hauf boattle a whisky thin two ir three boattles a magic, bit no auld Erchie. Anywey – nice tae be nice – evry man tae his ain, comes ten in we wint roon the coarnir tae git inty the wine. Auld Erchie waantit me tae go up tae his place bit Jesus Christ it's like annickers midden up there. So anywey A think A git aboot two moothfus oot it afore it wis done kis is A say whin auld Erchie gits stertit oan that plonk ye canny haud him. The auld cunt's a disgrace.

A left him it his close in wint hame. It wis gittin cauld in A'm beginnin tae feel it merr these days. That young couple wir in the close in aw, in it it is usual. Evry night i the week in A'm no kiddin ye! Thir parents waant tae gie thim a room tae thirsel, A mean evrybody's young wance – know whit A mean? They waant tae git merrit anywey. Jesus Christ they young yins nooadays iv goat thir heid screwed oan meer thin we ever hid, in the sooner they git merrit the better. Anyhow is usual they didny even notice me. It's Betty Sutherland's lassie in young Pete Craig – A knew his faither in they tell me he's almost is hard is his auld man wis. Still they've been winchin noo fir near enough six months so mibby she's knoaked some sense inty his heid. Good luck tae thim, A hope she his. A nice wee lassie – aye in so wis her maw.

A hid tae stoap two up fir tae git ma breath back, A'm no is bad is A wis bit A'm still no right; that bronchitis – Jesus Christ A hid it bad – hid tae stoap work cause ay it. Good joab A hid in aw oan the long distince. Landit up in the Western Infirmary way it tae. Murdir it wis. Still A made it tae the toap, A stey in a room in kitchen in inside toilet in it's no bad kis A only pey six in a half a month fir rent in rates. Bit A hear thir comin doon although A hope it's no fir a while kis A'll git buggir aw bein a singil man. If she wis back A'd git a coarpiration hoose bit she's gone fir good in anywey they coarpiration hooses urny worth a fuck. End up peyin a haunfil a week in dumped oot somewherr in the wilds? Naw! No me. No even a pub ir buggir aw? Naw they kin stick thim.

Wance in the hoose A pit oan the kettle fir a pot a tea in picked up a book. A'm no much ay a sleeper it times in A sometimes end up readin aw night. Aboot hauf an oor later the door goes. Funny! A mean A dont git that minny visitirs.

Anywey it wis jist young Tony who'd firgoat his key, wi that wee mate a his in a perr a burds. Christ whit dae ye dae? Invite thim in? Well A did – nice tae be nice – in anywey thir aw right they two; sipposed tae be a perr a terraways bit A ey fun Tony aw right in his mate's his mate. The young yins ir aw right if ye lea thim alane. A've eywis maintained that. Gie thim a chance fir fuck sake! So A made thim it hame although it meant me hivvin tae sit oan a widdin cherr kis A selt the couch a couple a months ago kis ay that auld cunt Erchie in his troubles. They four hid perred aff in wir sittin oan the ermcherrs. They hid brung a cerry-oot wae thim so A goat the glesses oot in it turned oot no a bad wee night, jist chattin away about politics in the hoarses in that. A quite enjoyed it although mine you A wis listenin merr thin A wis talkin bit that's no unusual. Wan i the burds didny say much either in A didny blame her kis she knew me although she didny let oan. See A used tae work beside her man – aye in she's nae chicken, bit – nice tae be nice – she isny a bad lookin lassie in A didny let oan either.

Anywey must a been near wan whin Tony gits me oan ma ain in asks me if they kin aw stey the night. Well some might a thought they wir takin liberties bit it the time it soundit reasonable. Course A said aw right in they could sleep ben the room in A'd sleep here in the kitchen. Tae tell the truth A end up spennin the night here in the cherr hell iv a loat these days. Wan minit A'm sittin readin in the nix it's six a cloak in the moarnin in ma neck's is stiff is a poker ir somethin. A've been thinkin iv movin the bed frae the room inty the kitchen recess anywey – might is well – A mean it looks hell iv a daft hivvin wan double bed in nothin else, aye in A mean nothin else sep the lino. Flogged every fuckin thin thit wis in the room in A sippose if A wis stuck A could flog the bed. Comes tae that A could even sell the fuckin room ir it least rent it oot. They Pakies wid jump it it – A hear they sleep twinty handit tae a room in mine's is a big room. Still good luck tae thim, they work hard fir thir money in if they dont good luck tae thim if they kin git away wi it.

A goat a couple a blankets in that bit tae tell the truth A wisny even tired. Sometimes whin A git the taste i that bevy that's me – awake tae aw oors. A've goat tae read then kis thir's nae point in sterrin it the waw – nothin wrang wi the waw right enough, me in Tony done it up last spring aye in done no a bad joab tae. Jist the kitchen bit kis A didny see the point i daen up the room wi it only hivvin wan double bed fir furniture. He pit up a photy a Jimi Hendricks oan the waw, a poster. A right big yin.

Whit's the story wi the darkie oan the waw? says auld Erchie, whin i came up the first time efter it wis aw done. Wis the greatest guitarist in the World ya auld cunt: says Tony in grabs the auld yin's bunnet in flings it oot the windy: First time A've seen yir heid: he says: Nae wunnir ye keep it covered.

Erchie wisny too pleased. Hidny seen him wioot that bunnet much masell. He's git two ir three strans i herr stretchin frae the back i his heid tae the front. The bunnet wis still lyin therr in the pavement whin he wint doon fir it. Even the dugs widny go near it. It's a right dirty lookin oabject bit then so's the auld yin's heid.

A drapped aff eventually wi oot chinegin – well it wid be broo day the morra in A waantit ay git up early wi them bein therr in that. Anywey mibby it wis the bevy A don't know bit the nix thin Tony's pullin ma erm, staunin oor me wi a letter frae the tax in A could see it wisny a form tae fill up. A'd nae ideer whit it wis so A opind it right away in oot faws a cheque fir forty-two quid. Jesus Christ A near collapsed. A mean A've been oan the broo fir well oor a year in naebody gits money eftir a year. Bit therr ye ur – forty-two quid tae prove me wrang. No bad eh?

Wiv knoaked it aff Stan! shouts Tony, grabbin it oot ma haun.

Well A mean A've seen a right few quid in ma day whit wi the hoarses in that bit it the time it wis like winnin the pools. Really wis! Some claes in mibby try fir that new HGV yiv goat tae git noo afore ye kin drive the long distance. Anywey Tony gits his mate in the burds up in tells thim it's time tae be goin in me in him wint doon the road fir a brekfast.

We wint inty the City Bakeries in hid the works in Tony boat a *Sporting Chronicle* in we dug oot a couple. Well he did kis A've merr ir less chucked it these days, aye long ago, disny bother me much noo bit in wan time A couldny walk past a bettin shop. Anywey nae merr i that, Tony gammils enough fir the baith i us. Course he'd bet oan two flies climbin a waw wherras A wis ey a hoarsey man. Wance ir twice A took an intrist in a dug bit really it wis eywis the hoarses wi me. A sippose the gammlin wis the real reason the wife fuckt aff in left me although ye definitely canny blame her – A mean she stuck it fir near thirty years. Anywey nae merr i that. A hid it aw figirt oot how tae spen it. Tony wint fir his broo money bit A decidet tae lea mine a week in case ay emergincies, in jist wint hame.

Whin A goat therr big Moira wis in daen the cleanin up fir me bit she wisny long in pittin oan a pot i tea. Jist aboot evry time ye see her she's either drinkin tea ir jist aboot tae pit it oan. So wir sittin in she's bletherin away good style aboot her weans in the rest ay it whin aw if a sudden she tells me she's gittin threw oot her hoose – aye in her four kids wi her. Said she goat a letter tellin her.

Canny dae it: A says.

Aye kin they no jist: says Moira: the coarpiration kin dae whit they like Stan.

Well A did know that is a matter i fact bit A also knew thit they widny throw a singil wummin in four weans oot inty the street bit A didny tell her that in case she thoat A wis oan therr side. Big Moira's like that – a nice lassie, bit she's ey gittin thins inty her heid aboot people so A said nothin. She telt me she wint up tae Clyde Hoose tae see the manager bit he wisny therr so she seen this young filla who telt her she'd hivty git oot in it wisny cause ay her debt (she owes thim a score back rent) naw it seems two ir three ay her neighbours wir up complainin boot the weans makin a mess in the close in shoutin in bawlin, ir somethin.

In thir's nothing ye kin dae aboot it noo: he says tae her.

Well that wis a diffrint story in A wis beginnin tae believe her. She wis aw fir sortin it oot wi her neighbours bit A telt her no tae bother until she fun oot fir sure thit thir wis nae reprieve. Anywey she wint away hame efter gittin the weans aff her maw. So Moira hid tae git oot her hoose afore the end ay the month, course whether they'd cerry oot thir threat ir no wis a diffrint story. Surely the publicity alane wid pit thim aff? A must admit the merr A thoat aboot it the angrier A wis becomin. Naw – nice tae be nice – ye canny go aboot pittin the fear i death inty folk – speshly the wummin. Moira might be a big lassie bit she's nae man tae back her up in whin it comes tae talkin they bastirts up it Clyde Hoose wid run rings roon her. Naw A know whit like it is masell kis A've hid ma run-ins doon it that broo aye in in it that National Assistance tae. Aye treat ye like A dont know whit in therr. A wis gittin too worked up so A picked up a book tae firget it fir a while. Anywey A fell asleep in the cherr – oot like a light in didny wake up tae near enough hauf past seven. Ma neck wis helluva stiff bit A didny bother wi the tea kis thir wis only a couple a oors tae go. A pit the coat oan in wint doon the road.

The Anchor wis crowded in A saw auld Erchie staunin near the domino table wherr he usually hings aboot if he's skint, in case emdy waants a drink – he sometimes gits a drink fir gaun. A wint straight tae the bar in assed Sammy fir two gless a whisky in a couple a hauf pints in whin A went tae pey the man A hid fuck aw bit some smash in a note sayin 'Give you it back tomorrow, Tony'. Forty quid in aw! A'll gie ye it the morra! Fuckin cheek! Probly oor it Ashfield the noo daen the lot in. Forty notes! Well well well – in it wisny the first time. A mean he disny let me doon, he's eywis goat it merr ir less whin he says he wid bit – nice tae be nice – know what A mean? See A gave him a sperr key whin we wir daen up the kitchen in let him hang oan tae it efterwirds kis sometimes he's nae wherr tae sleep in A let him kip wi me. Moira's maw his the other sperr yin tae let Moira in tae dae the cleanin up. Bit Tony drapped me right in it therr. Sammy's staunin therr, sayin nothin while A'm readin the note. The order comes tae aboot seventy pence in A've only git six bob in change. A whispers sorry tae Sammy in tells him A've come oot wi oot ma money.

Right Stan, it's aw right, A'll see ye the morra. Don't worry aboot it: says Sammy lookin at me.

Well it wisny bad ay him bit then A've bin inty him fir plenty wance ir twice before in it's eywis bin therr whin A said it wid. A mean – nice tae be nice – somebody's good enough tae gie ye it you be good enough tae gie it back – know whit A mean?

A gave the auld yin his drink in went in sat by massell. Tae be honest A didny feel in the mood fir either Erchie's patter or the dominoes. Forty sovvies! Naw the merr A thoat aboot it the merr A knew it wis oot i order. Aw he hid tae dae wis wake me up in A'd iv gied him the fuckin money. Mibby kept a haunfill masell bit A'd iv gied him the rest. Bit naw he took it. Still he must iv needed it pretty bad ir he widny iv. Bit the daft bastirt'll dae somethin stupit tae git it back, if he does it aw in it the dugs. Aw the worries ay the day whit wi big Moira in the weans gittin chucked oot in noo young Tony. Whit happens if they dae git chucked oot bit? Naw A canny see it. Possible bit! Might take a walk up Clyde Hoose masell in see whit it's aw aboot. A kin talk whin A waant tae bit right enough whin they bastirts up therr git stertit they end up blindin ye wi science. Anywey A git inty Sammy fir a haunfill oan the strength i ma double broo money nix week, in wint hame early wi a hauf boattle in a big screwtap bit A didny tell auld Erchie.

Tony still hidny showed up by the Monday, that wis four days in A knew fine he widny till he hid the forty sovvies. It wis obvious he wid hiv tae go tae the thievin gemms tae, in A didny waant that bit how dae ye tell thim? A've tried tae A'm blue in the face – in anywey it'd be too late kis he wid hiv the money the nix time A saw him.

Big Moira came doon oan Tuesday mornin wi a letter sayin she'd definitely hiv tae be oot the hoose by the thertieth ir else they'd take 'immediate action'. She wis in a helluva state in so wis her maw kis she couldny take thim, wi her only hivvin a single-end. A offered, bit a room in kitchen isny much better even though A've goat an inside toilet. Still A sippose it id dae it a pinch. Anywey A wint roon is minny factors is A could tae try in git her a hoose bit nae luck. Nothin! Nothin at aw. Ach A didny ixpect nothin anywey – A mean a singil wummin wi four weans, ye kiddin? Naw it wis hopeless so A telt her maw A'd go up tae Clyde Hoose in see if they'd offer alternit acco-midation, in no tae worry kis they'd never throw thim inty the street. Singil wummin in four weans? Naw the coarpiration widny chance it. A'd ixplain the situation aw right. Imagine ixpectin her tae pey a fiver a week anywey! It's beyond a joke. In she says the rooms ir damp tae, in whin she cawed in the sanitry they telt her tae open the windaes in let in the err. Open the windaes in let in the err? November? Aye in is soon is she turns her back aw the villains ir in screwin the meters in whit no. A wis ragin in whin A left the hoose in Wedinsday mornin A wis still helliva angry. Moira waantit tae come up wi me bit A telt her naw.

So A wint up tae Clyde Hoose in queued up tae see the manajir bit he wisny available so A saw the same wan Moira saw, a young filla cawed Mr Frederick. A done ma best tae ixplain bit he wisny botherin much in afore A'd finished he butts in sayin that in the furst place he'd ixplained evry thin tae Mrs Donnelly (Moira) in the department hid sent her two letters – in the second place it wis nane i ma business in then he shouted:

Nix please!

Will A loast ma rag it that in the nix thin A know A'm lyin here in that wis yesterday – Thursday – A'd been oot the gemm since A grabbed the snidey wee clerk by the throat. Lucky A didny strangil him tae afore A collapsed.

Dont even know if A'm gittin charged in tae be honest A couldny give two monkeys whither A um ir no. Bit that wis nothin, Moira's maw comes up tae visit me this mornin in tells me the news. Seems young Tony gits back Wedinsday dinner time lookin fir me bit no finein me goes roon tae Moira's maw who tells him the story. He says nothin tae her bit he wint away in goes straight up tae Clyde Hoose wherr he hings aboot till he fines oot who Mr Frederick is; then whin Mr Frederick goes hame a gang i thugs ir sipposed tae iv set aboot him in done him up pretty bad bit the polis only manajis tae catch wan i them in it turns oot tae be Tony who disny even run aboot wi emdy sep sometimes wee Shuggy. Anywey seems they'll lay it heavy oan him kis 'this type of young ruffian must be kept in check'.

So therr it is in A willny really know the score tae A see young Tony again. Bit it's Moira in the weans, is far is A know they've still nae wherr tae go. A mean – nice tae be nice – know whit A mean?

*James Kelman photographed in 1973 for* The Scotsman *newspaper. The caption read: 'I live in a slum and drink in pubs.'*

# Off the Buses

An interview with James Kelman by Anne Stevenson,
originally published in *The Scotsman*, 14 July 1973.

I met Jim Kelman over a pint in a crowded pub near Garioch
Mill Road in Glasgow, where he lives with his wife and two
small daughters. Jim's first book of short stories, *An Old Pub
Near the Angel*, has just been published in the United States by
the Puckerbrush Press of Orono, Maine; so it seemed appro-
priate to talk to him over a hubbub of voices and the acrid
smell of smoke and spilled beer.

Quiet spoken, fair, with large, expressive eyes, Jim considers
himself a Glaswegian, although after being brought up in
Drumchapel he has lived in California, London, Jersey and
Manchester. I asked him if the material for his stories, most of
which are about working-class people and written with excep-
tional depth and tenderness, was provided by his own life.

'Yes,' he said. 'I want to write about real people, real things.
I'm not interested in theories. A story can only be real if written
through your own experience.'

We were surrounded by university students, celebrating their
release from exams; so I asked him whether he thought a
university education would be of much help to his writing.

'No, not at all. I don't think anyone should go to university
before at least 25.' (Kelman is 27.)

'They don't know enough. It's training them to be officers
before they've learned to be men.'

'But you, yourself? Do you think now you'd like more education? Would you go to the university as a mature student?'

'Me? No. I don't write for educated people particularly. Of course I'm interested if they read my books, but I'm also interested in their reasons.'

'Who do you write for, then?'

'People,' he said. 'Ordinary people who might pick up the book on a news stand. Of course, I don't expect many people will pick up this book because they don't know about it. Half the booksellers I've approached won't take it. It's published in Maine by a small press and is only known by other writers. Writers are classless, or should be.'

'And yet you write mainly about working-class people.'

'I write about the working classes because I was brought up in a working-class family. I'm published in America because an American writer, Mary Gray Hughes, liked my stories. She couldn't have known anything about working-class Glasgow. I feel I have a lot in common with black writers who have to write from the point of view of class. They can't do otherwise. But that doesn't mean you write for a class, if you write about it.'

'I see what you mean,' I said. 'Tell me about your family and schooling. What made you want to write stories?'

'I was born in Govan, but we moved to Drumchapel, Number One Scheme, in 1954. My father is a craftsman, a picture framer known to Glasgow artists, and he taught me to know good workmanship.

'Drumchapel was a good place for a child to grow up, lots of fresh air and space. My brother was at a school in Hyndland, so I went there too. That was before there was a school in Drumchapel.

'I left school at 15 to be an apprentice printer and was a member of the printers' union. Then my father moved with the family to Pasadena, near Los Angeles in California. He thought there would be opportunities there, but after a while he got to hate the American system – master/slave relationship he called it – so he came back to Glasgow.

'Two of my brothers stayed in the US, but I returned with my father. We didn't have much money. The printers' union wouldn't have me back, so I went to work for a shoe factory in Govan. Then I was a sales assistant, a storeman and twice a bus conductor.

'In 1965 I went to Manchester where I worked in factories, occasionally doing 12-hour shifts, six days a week. I remember working a straight 20-hour shift once. It didn't pay very well.

'In 1967 I came back to Glasgow and worked on the buses until August of that year, when I headed for London. There I worked as a porter and on building sites and other things. For a while I picked potatoes in Jersey. Eventually I had to do a moonlight from there back to London.'

'Where you met your wife?'

'Yes, we met in 1969. Marie's from Swansea, a secretary. Shortly after we met, we married, and when we found she was going to have a baby we came back to Glasgow.'

'Why?'

'Accommodation's cheaper. We couldn't have afforded to live in London. I was working on the buses until last year, when I stopped and went on the buroo so as to have more time to write.'

'And you've wanted to be a writer all your life?'

'Well, no, I wanted to be a painter, but I wasn't good enough. I must have been 21 or two when I wrote my first stories. One was called "He Knew Him Well", about an old man who died without anyone knowing him. Another was called "Abject Misery", about having no money and no job.'

'Those are included in your book, aren't they? I've noticed quite a number of your stories take place in slums or pubs.'

'That's because I live in a slum and drink in pubs.'

'When did you begin to take your writing seriously?'

'It was in 1971. Philip Hobsbaum was giving an extra-mural class in creative writing at Glasgow University. I went along. He liked my work and encouraged me. When the American writer Mary Gray Hughes visited Glasgow last year he showed her my work.'

I asked finally about his plans for the future.

'I've no fixed plans. I'll probably keep writing, though I have to get a job again in January. My wife's supporting us now, but in January it'll be my turn. I can't write for television or radio. I'll keep writing stories. I began a novel last year and had about 60,000 words down on paper, but it turned out wrong. I've started another'

'Aren't stories difficult to get printed?' I suggested. 'Wouldn't it make sense to write for the media, since they pay well?'

'Media isn't real,' Jim replied. 'If I had to write something not real I'd drive buses again. Does that sound ridiculous?'

'I don't think so. What writers do you like then?'

'Mostly contemporary Americans. Mostly American women writers. Especially, I think, Katherine Ann Porter, Flannery O'Connor, Mary Gray Hughes and Tillie Olsen. But of course, men too. Sherwood Anderson, Isaac Singer. The Russian, Isaac Babel.'

'For somebody without a formal education you seem to have read quite a bit,' I said.

'You don't need a formal education to read,' Jim said.

We drank to that.

# Afterword

In the spring of 1973 a postman arrived at our door with a big parcel, a cardboard box containing 200 copies of *An Old Pub Near the Angel*. This was payment for my first collection of stories. We were living in a room and kitchen in Garriochmill Road. I ripped the parcel apart and showed the books to Marie and our infant daughters Laura and Emma. They were mightily impressed. At the back of four next morning I resumed paid employment and drove a bus out of Partick Garage. A time-inspector punished me for running six minutes sharp on a 64 bus through Brigton Cross. I explained that I was a writer and showed him a copy of the book. He thought it looked the part. In those days I carried a copy in case somebody wanted to read it.

*An Old Pub Near the Angel, and Other Stories* was published by Puckerbrush Press of Orono, Maine, U.S.A. It was a one-woman operation specialising in poetry but open to short fiction. Constance Hunting was the woman. Her publication of my work came about through a sort of fluke. She was shown it by the American poet and short-story writer Mary Gray Hughes whom I had met in Glasgow the year before.

I was fortunate to meet a few generous older writers (and readers) when I was younger. One was poet and critic Philip Hobsbaum. Another was the poet Anne Stevenson, daughter of American philosopher Charles Stevenson and biographer of Sylvia Plath. She and Philip were partners at that time.

Philip's influence on the literary scene of the period has been attested. He was a founder member of the group of poets known as 'the Movement' in late 1950s London. Others in the group included Pete Porter, John Redmond and Edward Lucie-Smith. In the mid 1960s he lectured at Queen's University, Belfast and around him gathered a group of younger writers that included Michael and Edna Longley, Seamus Heaney and Bernard MacLaverty. He became a senior lecturer at the University of Glasgow in the late 1960s and stayed for the rest of his days. In his spare time he tutored a weekly Creative Writing class for the Extra-mural Department. I attended this class during the 1971–2 academic year unless shiftwork made it impossible – one week early, one week late, and as much overtime as possible – but the class had become the highlight of my week and I was there at least once a fortnight.

It was a large class. Each session centred on the work of one or more of those present. Philip chaired the sessions. He would have had our stuff photocopied and ready for distribution the previous week. Thus people had at least seven days to study the poetry or stories properly. It was a good and thorough method. I was 25 and had been writing for three years. When it came my turn I passed five stories on to him.

This was the second time I had shown my work to anyone other than Marie. We had met in London not long after I started writing, in early 1969; she was twenty, a Swansea girl. I had begun writing only a few weeks before, and planned on returning to the U.S.A. where I had lived for a spell in my teens. I was in touch with the U.S. Embassy, had completed most of the paperwork and it appeared a formality.

Thereafter I forgot about it. Marie's dowry comprised four albums; Nina Simone, Los Paraguayos, the seminal *What is Soul?* anthology, and the fourth was by The New Seekers for which she makes no apologies. My one and only album which I won in a game of cards was the 1964 Newport Folk Festival recording featuring Boozoo Chavis, Doc Watson, the Swan Silvertones and old Fred McDowell. Only the New Seekers album is missing from our current collection but dastardly practices were not involved.

All my early stories were written in longhand until 1971 when I purchased an elderly desktop typewriter. Then I used both techniques. I have longhand drafts of stories as late as 'Nice to be Nice' and 'Remember Young Cecil'. Then we got a neat little portable typewriter that chased itself across the table when I pounded the keys. Occasionally Marie typed out the stories. She would not disclose if she read them. It is better not to show work to family and friends if you seek critical comment, as a general principle. I learned that from Marie. She earned a living as a shorthand typist and was very efficient. Efficient shorthand typists scan thoroughly but do not necessarily read. She gave me a certain look if I asked. Yet over the years I have heard her muttering 'Fair do's and all that pish'. This very line can be found in the first story I ever wrote and finished: 'Abject Misery'. She denies she got it from me. Maybe I got it from her.

Philip Hobsbaum photocopied and distributed my five stories to the other class members. On the night he said I should select three and read them. I had expected him to choose. I read 'He Knew Him Well', 'Abject Misery' and cannot remember the third.

At these sessions a critique of the work followed the reading. Philip chaired the sessions and avoided talking too soon, otherwise his contribution would have shaped the discussion. His way allowed class members to go off on their own. When the poem or story was being read he spent the time gazing over the top of his spectacles, watching the class. Maybe he saw me watching him.

After my reading came the critique. I enjoyed hearing people discuss my stories but certain aspects began to irritate me. I appeared to be absent. 'What Kelman should do is this.' 'No, instead he should do that . . .' 'Oh but what if he . . .'

Occasionally textual suggestions were made as though they never would have occurred to me. There was a vague assumption that the stories had just come. All I did was write them down. It was weird. I sweated blood over the damn things. Seventeen years later my novel *A Disaffection* was shortlisted for prizes and a member of an adjudicating panel asked if I ever revised 'or did it just come out?'

It jist comes oot, ah says, it's the natchril rithm o the workin klass, ah jist opens ma mooth and oot it comes. Similar to the American dancer in reply to a related question, ah jes closes ma eyes an ma feets git to movin.

Some of what I encountered from those early days prepared me for later struggles. But the blatant elitism encountered by so-called working-class writers still surprises me. I can never predict it. I assumed that anybody who thought about art and writing would know that my finished work was hard won.

During the session at Philip's class there were lapses in the conversation, fewer people took part. Maybe some were intimidated, not only by the language of the stories but by the subject matter. It was not the stuff of literature and they were peeved, but they remained silent; I think because there had been a very positive response from Philip and at least two others.

Philip entered the discussion earlier than usual. He read aloud from 'He Knew Him Well'. He was good at accents, in particular that of South London where for a couple of years he taught secondary school. It was an odd experience hearing somebody else speak the words and sentences so familiar to me. He brought to life the old man of 'He Knew Him Well'. It sparked ideas. It was exciting.

Later it became clear that for some in the class my work had been an ordeal. Hostile comments arrived. A letter came from a schoolteacher of English with an antipathy to 'the language of the gutter'. She found my stories disgusting and unreadable and did not see why they should have been forced upon her. She and her friend were among the small number who left the class never to return.

But why had they come in the first place? They had had a week to read the stories. They knew what to expect. Or did they? Perhaps they were there for the kill.

Philip was upset by their reaction. I assumed he would treat it ironically. Instead he took it seriously; he worried how it might affect me. It is true that I was unprepared. But equally I had been unprepared for his pleasure in the stories. At that time I was not prepared for much. It was my first experience of the world of letters – any response was noteworthy. I felt quite confident in what I was doing. In the face of the school-teacher's outrage there was little to be done other than give up writing, which by then was impossible.

Anyway, the negative stuff was insignificant in the face of one simple truth: Philip Hobsbaum, a real writer, had enjoyed my stories.

I have heard criticism of Philip over the years but he loved literature. Young writers did not scare him; he was not in compe-tition and was generous towards them. Philip made me feel like a real writer.

Although he showed me the English teacher's letter he did not give me it to keep. I speak from a distance of 35 years. She must have been hurt by something deeper than my five stories. Perhaps it was Philip's response that provoked her. He was supposed to be an authority. She and others would have consid-ered him a guardian not only of English Literature but of Standard English literary form. He could give that impression. He had the speech and mannerisms of a Cambridge professor.

Yet Philip spent much of his boyhood in a working-class Yorkshire environment, and was Jewish. He knew how to assimilate: sometimes he did, other times not.

I had no experience of higher education and English Literature as a field of study but was used to discussing books and writers with various people in my various jobs since leaving school. Friends, family and workmates shared information. I read voraciously and wrote whenever possible. I never thought about my writing as part of anything. If it was I hoped it might include Albert Camus, Franz Kafka and Fyodor Dostoevski. I had read a great many English-language writers but none had made such impact.

After Philip's class some of us walked down the road to the Rubaiyat Bar at the corner of Byres Road and University Avenue, to continue the conversation. It was a long way home but who cared about that. And I had company for much of the walk, a colleague from the class, John Roy, who was a poet and member of the Socialist Workers Party. I was always interested in horse racing. He was antagonised when I asked what happened to horse racing after the revolution. I thought it a fair question, he thought it frivolous. What has horse racing got to do with anything?

Ah well, nay S.W.P. for me. Sir Ivor, Vaguely Noble and Nijinsky had by then retired to stud but Mill Reef, My Swallow and Brigadier Gerard had exploded onto the scene. Heady days. Their exploits got me through many a weary shift.

In the Rubaiyat Bar Philip introduced us to a few of his acquaintances, including Donald Saunders, Alasdair Gray, Catriona Montgomery and Aonghas MacNeacail. Later he and Anne Stevenson would set up a small, independent writers' group at their home, by invitation. The four writers mentioned came along. It took place on a Sunday evening and operated in a similar format to the Creative Writing class but was separate from it. Other participants were Chris Boyce, Angela Mullane and Angus McAllister. Tom Leonard and Liz Lochhead were friends of some who attended but they did not appear until later, and not on a regular basis. I did not know them or their work. Tom and his wife Sonya were living in London at that time. After a year or so the group faded and by then I had stopped attending the extra-mural class.

Robin Hamilton was another poet who went to Philip and Anne's group. He wrote poetry and had connections with *Eboracum*, a literary magazine published by students at the University of York. On my behalf he submitted the story 'Nice to be Nice' for publication. It was accepted but caused the students a major headache. Their printer was a fundamentalist Christian who refused to print the magazine unless they withdrew my story. He said it was blasphemous and obscene, and tried to convince other York printers to reject the job. He succeeded with most but not all. The students stayed with the battle and eventually *Eboracum* was published, my story included.

'Nice to be Nice' was my earliest attempt at the literary or phonetic transcription of a speaking voice. It so happens that the voice belongs to a working-class man from Glasgow. The story is told in the 'I-voice', a first-person narrative. It was difficult to do. I spent ages working on it but learned much from the process.

It was one of the stories I later sent to Mary Gray Hughes. By then Philip Hobsbaum had passed her several. Early in 1972 she had visited the country from the U.S.A. She and Anne Stevenson had been close friends since student days. Both spent a year at Oxford. Anne and Philip held a wee night for her in their flat in Wilton Street. I talked to her the whole evening. I connected with her as a writer and it was an uncommon experience.

Mary Gray Hughes was a poet and short-story writer born in Brownsville, Texas, then living in Evanston, Illinois with her husband John, an economist. Her first collection of stories, *The Thousand Springs* (1971), had just been published by Constance Hunting's Puckerbrush Press. Any writer who knew her work held her in esteem. When she returned to the U.S.A. she passed my stories on to Constance who took a chance on them. So that was how, in the spring of 1973, my first collection of stories came to be published in Orono, Maine.

Mary Gray and I communicated regularly, exchanged work, recommended writers. She commented on my early stories, and it was important to me, even if I disagreed with some of it. She was a real artist. She advised caution in my use of 'dialect', and warned me of the risk of alienating the reader. This was directed at the title story of my first collection, 'An Old Pub Near the Angel'. But I saw in her comment that she had confused a piece of nonsense. At one point in the story the young central character, Charles, leaves the pub to buy a racing paper. When he returns he encounters an old lady at a table who 'sucked her gums and smiled across at him, then looked up at the barman. "Goshtorafokelch," she said.'

Mary Gray thought 'Goshtorafokelch' was a failed attempt at a localised London dialect. It was not. I meant it like it is. The old lady may or may not be a Londoner. What she says is indecipherable to Charles. Of more fascination to him is her 'gums', and that she is 'around 90 years old'. By that time he has swallowed a couple of beers, in the process of spending his ill-gotten gains from a wrongful payout at his local broo. He has just come from signing on at the old unemployed register formerly located on Penton Street across from Chapel Market. I did many a weary trudge from there myself, then back to

Calthorpe Street WC1. In earlier versions of that story I alter-
nated between a first and third-person narrative. I did the same
with 'Abject Misery' and 'Dinner for Two'.

Mary Gray recommended I look at the work of Flannery
O'Connor and Emily Brontë's use of dialect in *Wuthering
Heights*. Of course I had my own opinions about 'dialect' and
in response to her comment on language I sent her 'Nice to be
Nice'. She replied, 'Forget all I said about dialect . . . you obvi-
ously know what you are doing better than anyone.'

In regard to my own stories I did feel that way. I was working
my way through things. I never bothered about alienating
readers, neither then nor now. The priority was to write the
story properly. The readers could take care of themselves. There
were a couple of editorial judgments made by Puckerbrush that
I allowed. I felt it was good manners to allow something. Editing
can become a negotiation between writer and editor. I am not
in favour of that. Editing is necessary but negotiation can imply
the presence of a third party: the marketing team. A couple of
alterations I allowed through I later regretted, but only mildly.

My original intention in 'Nice to be Nice' was to use the
phonetic transcription only for the narrative. I thought to apply
Standard English form for the dialogue. It was an attempt to
turn the traditional elitist assumption on its head. I was irritated by so-called working-class writers who wrote third-party
narratives in Standard English then applied conventional ideas
of phonetics whenever a working-class character was called
upon to say a few words. When a middle-class character entered
the dialogue all attempts at 'phonetics' disappeared; his or her
lines were transcribed in standard form, leading to the extraordinary presumption that Standard English Literary Form is a
literal transcription of Upper-Class Orature.

Others were less impressed by 'Nice to be Nice'. Some made
no attempt to read it. Of course the language made it difficult.

But so what? That just meant it was a difficult story. It was not a structural fault. I did not care if somebody did not read it. But I got weary with explanations. Read it or not, but there it is.

Some who knew Tom Leonard's work assumed I was familiar with his *Six Glasgow Poems*, published in 1969. These poems are brilliant. But why would people think I knew them? If I had, it would have affected my work, and that particular story would have been altered fundamentally. Tom's language was pared to the minimum, and his precision even then, at the age of 21 or 22, was all that any artist could have sought.

There was a particular response to 'Nice to be Nice' that irritated me, as though the struggle for the means of expression was definitive, that the battle had been won and the war was over. According to that argument, the primary concern is the means of expression: the thing expressed is irrelevant. Forget about the primacy of this story and that story and that one over there; this writer, that writer and the one over there. They admit the validity of the language, they do not want the poetry and stories. The language exists and people exist who use it, okay, but do not force them down our throat!

In 'Nice to be Nice' the story is narrated in the first person by the central character. I was concerned about other characters. There are four in all: the narrator; his old pal Erchie; the young fellow who exploits him; and the single mother in danger of losing her home. In what sense could the 'I-voice' be defined as the central character? Only because he is telling the story. Each of the four characters would see it differently, each of the four characters had their own story, a different story. I started writing them, each as a first-person narrative. The shift in the language of each person was the most interesting factor. That subtlety, the sophistication of how human beings use language, is not possible for the elitist or racist for whom working-class existence may be an amorphous experiential mass, but if you hear one you hear them all, see one you see them all. During the Booker Prize controversy of 1994 much of the hostility directed at *How Late It Was, How Late* derived from the astounding proposition that the life of one working-class Glaswegian male is a subject worthy of art. I was used to the prejudice but the gleeful abandon with which some attacked my work took me by surprise. It never occurred to the literary mainstream that working-class males from Glasgow might be watching the programme or reading the newspaper.

Ultimately there was only one story, 'Nice to be Nice'. I composed it as best I could. The other draft versions are in a bottom drawer someplace. But it was not my first story to appear in print. Glasgow University's Extra-mural Department had its own little magazine, edited by Ann Karkalas, and she published 'He knew him well' in early 1972.

Ann is another hero. During that period in the early 1970s she fostered contemporary writing in Glasgow and elsewhere. She sought different ways to do it, extending the range of the Extra-mural Department. She employed part-time tutors like myself to lead Creative Writing groups. It was only two hours a week for maybe ten weeks but for an artist any money is crucial. And money you earn as a result of your labours as an artist, that is fucking well nigh unique; it is just such an exciting thing, a validation. You run and show your family the cheque. Ann Karkalas took it for granted that we could lead these groups, and maybe bring to them some crucial element of our own.

When that shipment of 200 books arrived myself and Marie thought about their distribution. We gave many to family and friends. Occasionally I charged somebody £1.50 or £2. My grannie paid the dough without a grumble.

I asked friends what to do with them. Sell or deposit them in bookshops was the response. I walked along Great Western Road with a pile. A newsagent near Kersland Street gave me a cheery grin. He accepted three copies on a sale-or-return basis. Perhaps they sold. I never went back to check. I managed to place a few more in local bookshops. I returned to see if they had sold but generally no one knew. I had to content myself with a gentlemanly nod, departing with self-respect intact.

Somebody suggested I take a few to Edinburgh bookshops. I wondered what to wear. Should I adopt the bohemian look or that of the 'prosperous clerical worker'? Unfortunately, in those days I wore my hair long and had a beard so the 'prosperous clerical worker' image was tricky. I walked the middle path. I donned a duffle coat but wore a neat pair of trousers rather than jeans. I had discovered that clothes can be a problem for writers.

Years later I was with Tom Leonard and Alasdair Gray arriving to do a reading somewhere, and each of us wore a herring-bone-patterned Harris Tweed sports jacket. We were not taken aback. I think Alasdair said, Aha!

In the mid 1970s I was guest speaker (recommended by Ann Karkalas) at a writers' workshop on the Ayrshire coast, on my way to pick up two hours' work plus expenses. I guessed it would be a middle-class set-up and adopted the 'prosperous clerical worker' approach: dark overcoat, shirt and tie and the usual neat trousers. Months before I had cut off the long hair and shaved the beard off completely, so I looked well scrubbed. I also carried a bag. A bag! It might even have been a briefcase! Fuck sake man. Unfortunately the Bhoys were playing Ayr United away that evening in a cup tie, and the train was packed full of green-and-whites. I had to stand there. A couple of the Celtic fans noticed me; one pointed and shouted, Look at Elmer Fudd!

Fucking mortified man, I did not know where to look.

But he was quite right.

So, back in 1973, still with all the hair, I had donned the duffle coat and journeyed to Edinburgh with a bagful of *An Old Pub Near the Angel*. I walked to the first place on the list, up the hill from Waverley Station, James Thin's bookshop on South Bridge. Inside I wandered by the shelves, composing myself, bagful of books at the ready. I saw a smallish dome-headed personage who seemed to work in the place. He observed me. Maybe I was a book shoplifter. In those days I was a book shoplifter. If I had been engaged in that pursuit then he would not have spotted me.

I approached him. I asked about the set-up. Did a writer chap seek out the manager or what? I indicated my bag. He was wary to the point of fear and pointed towards the woman at the cashier desk. So I asked her. Oh, you should see Mister Thin, she said, pointing back the way. It was the same wee baldy guy. He was watching me. Now he backed away. I left the premises, for the next train back to Glasgow.

None of the people I knew earned much at all from writing – Aonghas MacNeacail, Tom Leonard, Liz Lochhead, Donald Saunders, Anne Stevenson, Alasdair Gray. Little bits of tutoring and the occasional paid reading, that was about it.

Mary Gray Hughes advised me, 'If you want to earn money, don't be a writer, at least not a "real writer" . . . [real] writing has a lot of grimness in it.' She never earned a thing from writing either. Like the rest of us she occasionally led Creative Writing classes or placed a story in a literary journal. Twenty years passed until our next meeting, which was in Chicago in 1995. We corresponded throughout the years, until her death from cancer in 1999. Constance Hunting published a posthumous collection of her stories in 2002 (*Cora's Seduction, and Other Stories*, Puckerbrush Press).

Mary Gray's father was Hart Stilwell, a radical Texan journalist and fiction writer from the first half of last century. When I taught a graduate class in Creative Writing in Austin, it took place in the old home of J. Frank Dobie, a legendary Texan man of letters (who corresponded with R.B. Cunninghame Graham). Hart Stillwell had studied at the University of Texas in Austin in the early 1920s. He knew J. Frank Dobie and visited his home on occasion. It was a rich coincidence for myself.

In 1992, after a gap of 19 years, Puckerbrush Press published the second edition of *An Old Pub Near the Angel* and it was twice reprinted. On the small-press scene that represents a bestseller. Although I received ten copies of the new edition I never did receive any money. Whenever Connie Hunting earned anything it was ploughed into the next publication, mainly local writers and poets from the area around Maine. I felt privileged to be part of it, as would any young writer. I never met her personally. I wish I had. She liked to keep in touch with her writers and got a kick out of seeing us move on. She died in April 2006 at the age of 80. She was one of the great literary figures in that small-press tradition and it is an honour to dedicate this reissue to her memory.

Although *An Old Pub Near the Angel* earned me no actual money there were indirect benefits. I applied for an Arts Council grant and was awarded £500. We used £400 of it as the deposit towards a two-bedroom flat in North Woodside Road, close by the old Pewter Pot. By then Tom Leonard and Liz Lochhead were both back living in Glasgow and I got to know them. Tom's first collection, *Poems*, appeared around the same time as *An Old Pub Near the Angel* in 1973. Liz's *Memo for Spring* had been published a year earlier.

When we moved into our new flat Tom and Alasdair Gray helped with the flitting. We just heaved the stuff round the corner. Liz was short of a place to stay and took over our old room and kitchen in Garriochmill Road. Unfortunately, no sooner had she moved in and Glasgow Corporation started knocking it down. Then a couple of years later they demolished, by compulsory purchase, our part of North Woodside Road. They gave us £1,500 and a council flat in lieu.

Living as an artist is another way of living on your wits unless you get a stroke of amazing fortune, such as marrying a breadwinner. Marie was that breadwinner. Following the end of one statutory spell on the broo I was forced to get a job. Driving buses was the only serious option. I had worked on the buses on six previous occasions and my last term included an unofficial strike to which I was closely connected, so it seemed like a long shot. But the transport official who interviewed me had a sense of humour. He knew of *An Old Pub Near the Angel* and remembered reading an interview Anne Stevenson did with me for *The Scotsman* newspaper. He gave me another chance. I nearly said 'with a twinkle in his eye'; fortunately I know better. Not only did I beat the odds, but my first collection of stories was paying its way; without it the buses would not have re-employed me.

In early 1974, however, I had to resign for good. I was going mad. A few months later old Partick Garage closed for the last time. I used its layout and location at the corner of Hayburn Street and Beith Street for my novel *The Busconductor Hines*.

Except for one copy, I have since disposed of all of that first edition of *An Old Pub Near the Angel*. This last copy is the one I sold my grannie. She was a big fan. After she died I nabbed it, but she would have wanted me to have it, and that is the truth.

My father, Ronald, had a workshop at the foot of the same tenement building where me, Marie and the kids lived. Like his father before him he was a self-employed picture-framer and gilder. His three older brothers were also in the trade. Many years ago a specialism within that trade was picture restoration but it was stolen by the bourgeoisie and transformed into their own intellectual property. Their Universities' Degree in Fine Art then became necessary to practise the work – by now termed a profession – within art and other state institutions, e.g. galleries and museums. The seven-year apprenticeship and a journeyman's continuous application at the trade were no longer sufficient qualification. A graduate student left university at 23 and entered straight into the 'profession'. For the last ten years of his working life my father took a job within an art institution as a gilder and frame-maker. It irked him that he was barred from restoration work; he gritted his teeth when the white-coated 23-year-old 'technician' asked him to move his elbows out of the way so s/he could get on with the 'fine' art.

A similar robbery is being attempted on the practice of literary art. The higher learning institutes have commandeered much of this, from Sydney to San Diego, Seattle, Boston, through London, Glasgow, Edinburgh and ever onward. The title they have applied to the activity is 'Creative Writing'. It is preferable that the practice engaged in by the students is not described as 'creating art'. That is too ambiguous, not only does it imply 'freedom', it suggests a distinction may be drawn between literary art and what they themselves practise.

Conformity, convention, homogeneity at all costs; arise Ye Standard English Literary Form. The values being stamped as a template within this field of endeavour, 'Creative Writing', act as though designed to destroy diversity. These values are not confined to the aesthetic.

In future, public areas associated with literary art – publishing, magazine editing, newspaper reviewing, bookselling etc., the entire range – will be controlled by the values of 'Creative Writing'. Much of it is already. Power lies with the priesthood: graduate students with degrees in a subject invented by their peers. In the past they had only Degrees in English

Studies. Now they can inform other 'Creative Writers' (i.e. literary artists) what they can and cannot do, not simply as editors and critics, but as editors, critics and fellow 'Creative Writers'.

Literary artists will still be able to fight. They will be able to do their work. Certain areas and markets will be closed off to them. It will become increasingly difficult for authentic writers to enter institutes of higher learning in a teaching capacity, not unless they have obtained a 'Degree in Creative Writing' and are equipped to teach students how to disguise their passions, conceal their emotions, dull their minds, push the self-destruct button on their imagination.

For generations Departments of English Studies and other language literatures have fought to pronounce the death of 'the artist', that and their own entitlement to a tenured position, the right to earn a lifetime's salary derived from the artwork produced by the deceased. Nowadays the one branch of the study that pays lip service to the human beings who create the stuff, 'Creative Writing', is slowly but surely having its life snuffed out from within, like a worker dying from the effects of asbestos fibre. People who die from this do not 'pass on'; the breath is squeezed from their lungs forever and ever, amen.

When I find myself within such an institution I feel like the character portrayed by Donald Sutherland in the movie about Zombies and Sunflower Plants, as I stroll across campus, trying to mask my self-consciousness, awaiting a bloodless body in a flowing black robe to halt in mid-stride, pointing me out to his colleagues in an accusatory shriek: Aaahhhh! Aaarrtist!

A hunner and fifty years ago, or thereabouts, Herman Melville suggested that two novels might exist for every one created; the unwritten one concerned the endeavours of the writer in the act of creating the damn thing. The horrible part of this is that Melville, as I recall, was silent for almost twenty years. Meanwhile in other parts of the world the literary texts of a handful of writers indicate that not only might they have shared Melville's insight, they were attempting to rectify matters. But what truly would have excited Melville was that these furnir literary artists were doing it simultaneously.

What furnir literary artists is he talking about?

Away and fucking read the fucking books.

The work of these artists is at the heart of what we call the 'existential tradition in literature'. Anglo-American institutions have difficulty with such furnir stuff.

Theorists of 'Creative Writing' have derived a 'holding tactic' to stem the nightmare: Graduate Students are now instructed that in order to qualify for the Jackie Wilson Degree in Creative Writing – ever Higher and Higher – they should submit a Final Paper that is a Critical Analysis of themselves in the act of creation; to what extent does their finished 'art product' match the original idea, conception or design?

Ah, excellent, an Anglo-American counterblast to the literary Enlightenment that allows a return to Shaftesbury and Alexander Pope, while sneaking in a neat wee argument for the existence of a Christian God – *a priori*, if we do our home-work. What more could be asked by academia?

Under the banner of 'Creative Writing' the Anglo-American higher education institutions have tried to corner the 'literary art market' for years, producing their own literary journals, anthologies of poetry and fiction, chosen from among them-selves, and fostered within academia as 'the good'. Nobody buys them apart from each other, but it does not matter, because the public pays for most of it, via state and/or government subsidy. Nevertheless, students are taught to recognise this work as 'the good'. Forget all that existential angst stuff, our society moves as one, with a sharply defined set of criteria. For all I know, 'Creative Writing' has its roots in a 1950s

CIA/MI6 propaganda project relating to literary arts and the suppression of debate generally. Certainly it bears the analytic stamp of that giant of the Anglo-American intellect, B.F. Skinner.

Fortunately there are academics who believe that a relationship exists between art and those who create it, that this may be protected and fostered, thus they fight to employ real writers.

Perhaps the defect is not yet structural, that it might be remedied by saturating these tiny departments with living breathing literary artists who can open a vein and offer students a drink. But the artists will not come if time and space is denied them. They will not come if the academics look enviously upon them, and demand that they share the full burden of bureaucratic and administrative necessity. And the artist must say to the academics, Fight yer own fucking war.

The 'literary art market' of the world cannot be controlled in the same way as they controlled my father's craft of picture restoration. Yet the irony is severe. They transformed his craft into a 'fine art'. They are transforming my art into a craft. Those dulled by institutionalised 'Creative Writing' are roused to excitement by talk of 'craft'. Students walk about arm-in-arm and with beatific smiles, bearing a striking resemblance to the duo who came finally for Josef K. Oh, they say, we are learning our craft. Do not talk to us about formal necessity or arguments from design; when we hear any of those we run for cover. Next year our Creative Writing Professor is taking a Sabbatical to follow up an idea he has for a Gothic Romance. But he may do a Literary Novel instead. His editor, a former M. Litt graduate student from our very programme, has asked him to outline a proposal, always remembering the subtle nuances of the literary market. But what about the one he discussed with us in class, about the Detective Chief of Police who continually flouts Political Authority but always gets his man through the powers of Ice-Cool Logic and his intimate knowledge not only of the underworld, but Early Victorian Fiction in Old London Town?

My father still received picture-restoration work in a private capacity. One of his personal customers was the Director of Kelvingrove Art Galleries, Dr Honeyman. Occasionally he and a pal made antiques (*sic*). His pal was a cabinetmaker to trade. At that time in Glasgow many of the city's cabinetmakers and French-polishers were employed around the Corunna Street area of Finnieston. Along Argyle Street were various crafts and antique shops. Different tradesmen could work on the same job. One fine cabinetmaker was Ben Smith, British champion racing cyclist. (By coincidence Ben Smith's daughter and her husband are now close friends of me and Marie.) My father always knew when he arrived by the sound of the cycle's handle-bars against the workshop window.

Craft-suppliers and related businesses were centred around the old Anderston Cross, and right the way along Stobcross Street was a range of carriers to transport your goods across the world. I tramped that whole area as a 15-year-old message-boy, carrying goods to the shipping offices and the carriers, the stamp and dyers, printers and machine-tool shops. It was my first job after leaving school. Like all young folk I walked to save busfares, servicing my tobacco and gambling habits. Myself and my elder brother were used to going business messages from schooldays. Usually it was to one of the wee private galleries and frame-makers around the Kelvinbridge and Charing Cross districts.

I am the second of five, all boys. We enjoyed poking about in Dad's workshop and he showed us how to burnish gold-leaf frames. Whatever we did, we must not sneeze or cough, otherwise flecks of gold scattered into the sawdust on the floor. He had all that great stuff beloved by boys and girls: oils and water-based paints; brushes; methylated spirit by the gallon; knives, glues and tools and tools and tools; and planks of fresh wood; and scores of frames and crazy ornate moulds from the early nineteenth century. Composition forever bubbled in strange little saucepans – the 'compo pots'. Old composition had solidified round the walls and over the edges of the saucepans. The 'compo recipe' was a closely guarded family secret. When times were tough and all else failed we ate it with a mixture of cod-liver oil and brown sauce. He used to offer customers a cup of tea but to their horror – Do you think I'm made of pots? – he boiled the water out the 'compo pot'.

Most of the old-time journeymen were meths drinkers; according to my father, the 'compo' put a lining in their stomach. When he was 15 his own father – my grandfather – employed on a casual basis an elderly picture-framer by the name of Jake, who was then hitting 80. Therefore he was born in the 1830s. I have his saw. But a pal of mine, Alistair Kerr, is not impressed by the saw. He is a joiner to trade and believes this mystique of the legendary skills of old-time tradesmen is romantic keech.

There were always old paintings and reproductions around in our family. My grandfather started the business, immigrating to Glasgow from Aberdeenshire around the turn of the twentieth century. It was a luxury trade. In times of depression business was scarce. If there was work on occasionally he needed other workers, usually his older sons. He hung exhibitions down south for private galleries, including the Annan which greatly impressed myself.

As a youth I was fond of van Gogh although his life did not excite me like that of others. I enjoyed reading about him but he was just too messianic for myself at that age, and his bad luck with women put me off. My opinion has changed. When

I taught a graduate class at the University of Texas I used his letters on art theory. All students of art should read his letters. But as a youth I knew well his portrait of Alexander Reid. I wondered if it was Mister Reid's hair that appealed to van Gogh. No matter, my grandfather shook the hand of the man who shook the hand of Vincent. I liked the idea of him and my uncles driving to London to hang an exhibition and, of course, that my middle name is Alexander.

But he could never build the picture-framing, gilding and restoring business sufficiently to employ more than one man and a boy on a regular basis. His older three sons sought work in other towns. My father was the baby of the family, by several years the youngest of six children, two of whom died in infancy. It was his own misfortune never to have worked alongside his three big brothers.

My grandfather took a part-time job as a door manager at the old Empire Theatre. His great pastime was music and he sang in one of Glasgow's choruses, so maybe he had contacts in show business. He still worked in a small way at the trade where possible. One customer was the artist J.D. Fergusson. His wife was Margaret Morris, a famed dancer and beauty of the day. She is the model Fergusson painted most frequently. Unfortunately my grandmother was sensitive to certain matters where Alexander was concerned. She thought his choral activities an excuse to meet other women. One night he got the family free tickets for a show, and when he was showing my grannie to her seat in the stalls there came a call from above, Yoohoo Sandy!

It was Margaret Morris from up in the boxes with J.D., dressed in the height of fashion. She stood up to wave down to my grandfather. And she used 'Sandy', his family name. My grannie never forgave him. Later they separated. My father was 12 at the time. He remained with his father, lodging in houses around Kelvinbridge. When the pair flitted from place to place the bulk of their belongings was choral songbooks. They had different workshops over the years; Partick Cross, Otago Street, Gibson Street and Great Western Road were some of the addresses. But he stayed in touch with his mother, and when we were growing up we visited her regularly. She was the last Gaelic speaker in my immediate family, Katherine MacKenzie from Kios on Lewis. Dizzie Gillespie's grannie was also a Gaelic speaker, from North Carolina, U.S.A.

Before the First World War picture-framers and gilders could be hired on a casual basis at the corner of Cadogan Street and Waterloo Street. Many art studios lay up Blythswood Hill, in the vicinity of the square, five or ten minutes from the Glasgow School of Art. Female models were traditionally hired from there by artists. The art models have been gone for nearly a century. From there and down the hill towards Argyle Street women continue to hire their bodies, but for the last many years they have risked horrific violence, including murder, selling themselves for sex.

In the 1950s Salvador Dali's painting, *Christ of Saint John of the Cross*, was vandalised by one of Glasgow's religious bigots inside Kelvingrove Art Gallery. Under Dr Honeyman's direction the gallery had purchased some very fine art, including the vandalised Dali painting. My father was one of the many with whom he discussed its restoration. I remember seeing other ripped, scarred and badly damaged canvases people brought into his Gibson Street workshop. In some of those paintings large areas were threadbare. Time and patience were required for these jobs. Eventually, and it could be several months later, he could show us where he had mended the canvas and applied the paint and whatever else was necessary. Note the clouds and the flock of geese. See that bush, these big waves. Look closely.

If it had been a very bad rip you might see something of the repair; otherwise not. Of course it was him that had painted the clouds, the bush and the flock of geese, matching the oils of the eighteenth-century original. That trade was full of stories.

One morning in the early 1970s Marie and I were walking along Sauchiehall Street and we stopped to read the notice for a forthcoming sale of Scottish paintings at the old Crown Auction Rooms. One of the artists whose work was to be auctioned was Alexander Kelman. I asked my father if he was a relation. He's your grandpa!

Whenever the signature disappeared from the face of a canvas during the restoration process one of the old-time journeymen signed their own name for a laugh. Some of these old paintings had been in and out of restoration so often that the only paint left on the canvas had been applied by the restorers.

My grandfather died in 1951. He is buried in his family lair along King Street, Aberdeen.


In my teens the biographies of artists of the late eighteenth and the nineteenth centuries were some of my favourite reading. I looked at reproductions of their work too. I enjoyed people like Dave, Ingres, Corot and Courbet; and Velázquez and Rubens; and, in particular the Impressionists and Post-Impressionists. My early heroes were Degas and Manet; afterwards Modigliani, Rodin, Cézanne and Utrillo; especially Rodin and Modigliani, flitting in and out of Parisian bars and coffee houses, never eating, swallowing dope and booze by the bucket, constant sex. Then they all met other artists for conversations over a bowl of Mrs Pissarro's homemade soup. What a life! I thought Modigliani's paintings of naked women were just superb and if anybody wanted to argue – well, I would just have argued back.

I assumed I would become a painter. Art was the only class

that interested me at school. My first proper art teacher, Mrs Harper, was strict but ironic, the best kind. She let us choose and sort out the materials for ourselves; charcoals, brushes, get our own water from the sink. To be granted such responsibility was an extraordinary experience. You were also allowed to talk to your classmates, females as well as males, as long as you kept it quiet and did not laugh too loudly.

Nevertheless, school proved too much for me even in the short run. I turned 15 and needed out. I returned to start a fourth year in August but those first days were a living night-mare. I had failed third year in the most miserable fashion so this fourth year was a repeat year. A careers teacher was seeing pupils so I took that opportunity to escape a double period of History which, as I recall, was devoted to the Exciting Adventures of the later Diaturnable Drones of Imperial England. I discov-ered I was out of cigarettes so went along to hear the careers teacher to pass the time. He asked if I was interested in anything. Art, I said.

Well, I have the very job for you.

The printing trade. A firm down the road in Partick was looking for a boy and my qualifications were spot on: Boys' Brigade and Protestant Senior Secondary School.

You did not have to be a Protestant to work in that printing shop but it got you entry into the better occupations. Protestants became compositors. Catholics did the labouring and semi-skilled work. If they made it as time-served journeymen it was to the level of machinemen, printers. They wore boiler-suits. The very idea. Compositors wore dustcoats.

A drawback to hourly paid work is how it crushes the spirit. First Year Apprentice Compositors had their own defences. If you were at your wits' end and desperate for a day off, you injected yourself with lead. You drew blood around the area of the wrist and rubbed in some of the fluid from the lead type, then waited to see if it 'travelled'. The thing that 'travelled' was poison. It ran a thin red streak up a vein in the inside of your forearm. It was great when it 'worked'. You showed the thin red stripe to the gaffer and he sent you home. But you were not to let the red line move beyond your elbow. If that happened it went right up and through your body and just was there and 'it' would not come out, thus one had breathed one's last, that was you, deid. You had to flex your upper-arm muscle as tautly as possible and grip your inside elbow very tightly. That stopped it.

My father and mother decided to emigrate with the family to the U.S.A. in 1963. They were in their early forties with five sons, aged from three to 20. My father advertised in different newspapers across the U.S.A. and received replies from around seven prospective employers, including Houston, Texas; Springfield, Missouri; and Hartford, Connecticut. Dr Honeyman had written his references. He and my mother chose Los Angeles, California, working for a private art gallery in Pasadena. A house went with the position. They gave myself and my elder brother, Ronnie, the choice to go or stay. I could finish my apprentice-ship – my other grandparents, my mother's parents over in Govan, offered me a place to stay – then emigrate later. To go with my family meant severing my apprenticeship, but it was an easy choice. Ronnie also decided quickly. He worked as a clerk for the old Glasgow Corporation and was glad to escape. Our younger brothers Alan and Philip were still at school while Graham, the youngest, was only three.

The secretary of the union, S.O.G.A.T. (the Society of Graphic and Allied Trades), advised me that it was a serious matter and amounted to voluntary expulsion. I would be finished with the trade in this country, except for non-union shops. But he wished me well and gave me a good letter of introduction for any printers interesting in hiring me.

On the day before we left I went into a bookie's at Partick Cross and stuck my entire life savings on a horse by the name of Pioneer Spirit. It won at 4/5. I got £9 back. Arkle and Mill House were around in them days. Sea Bird II had won the Derby.

Los Angeles proved an ordeal. I had been working for about two and a half years in Glasgow. Now I was in a country where at 17 I was too young to work. I went looking anyway, scouting about. Surely I would find something. My elder brother had found a job, earning real dollars.

In Pasadena they had a labour exchange office near Colorado Boulevard. I tried it a few times. A printing factory needed 'experienced men'. I took a chance and they gave me an interview. They knew of S.O.G.A.T. and were impressed by the secretary's letter. It was a non-union shop along Colorado Boulevard. In those days the non-union shops had their own sort of union or society. Their interview included practical work with the composing stick and a case of type. It was too easy for a Second Year Glasgow Apprentice and they were keen to start me. But I had to bide my time until my eighteenth birthday. There was nothing else for it, they had no choice. They said they would write me later. I continued trudging around Pasadena but there was little doing there. I began travelling into Los Angeles whenever possible. Surely some sort of under-the-counter job existed?

If there was I did not find it. My father and my elder brother were working; my two younger brothers at school; and my mother busy with all the domestic stuff, trying to make ends meet. I was company for her, kept my youngest brother from under her feet.

The money brought into the home by my elder brother was greatly appreciated. The cost of living was proving greater than anticipated. Our father's wage did not go as far as all that. He was finding difficult the transition from self-employed tradesman to wage-slave employee. At home he had worked nine, ten or twelve-hour days, six days a week, and if he was five minutes late, so what? One way or another he got the work done. Now he had to cope with the timecard routine. A minute late and people took notes. He was not there in the guise of the gruff but loveable Scottish engineer who can build a spaceship from a dod of chewing gum, three nuts and a bolt. He had expected to be treated as a first-class craftsman, but the gallery used him like any other worker. His workmates were from Puerto Rico and Central America. He was also an immigrant; immigrants are cheap labour.

Most of the time I read or loafed about. L.A. was where the jobs lay but it costs money to look for a job. That had to come from the family budget. Busfares mount up. If you are out for several hours, a coffee and a sandwich enter the reckoning. I could not borrow if I could not pay back. It was donations or nothing and nobody wants charity, not even 17-year-olds, especially ones that have been independent for years. You become overly sensitive. I hated to be 'caught reading'. But what else was there? I went out for walks but that area of Pasadena was fairly boring, besides which walkers were suspicious characters.

My mother made sandwiches for my father and elder brother. I took one when I travelled into the city, two or three times a week. Occasionally I walked to save money. It was 11 miles from Pasadena to downtown L.A. Coming home in the dark was worse, down across quite a wide stretch of railroad tracks and through Chinatown and then on, and on, and on.

I got to know the downtown area quite well. There was a single-window record store nearby a pawnshop whose entire window was devoted to Bob Dylan merchandise. This was a time for Elvis, the Everlys, Del Shannon, so it was an adventurous display. Back in Glasgow, Dylan had a cult following but only a hardy few; the rest of the population had succumbed months previously to The Beatles, myself included. I had the *Please Please Me* album and took it everywhere, until I lost it – I hope not at cards. Bob Dylan's image did not last long in that record-store window.

Like most other exiled teenagers I was proud when The Beatles stormed the U.S.A. In Glasgow there was also a music scene. We had good bands of our own: Blues Council and the Pathfinders were just two; a third was George Gallagher's The Poets. A couple of nights ago, as I write here in San José, January 2007, a local radio station featured two of their songs. It was a complete surprise, sitting staring out the window at 11 o'clock in the evening. I was expecting a wee lassie to jump out and shout, Ha ha Dad, April Fool!

The Poets split up in the 1960s. Individuals continued in other bands. In the 1980s some were doing gigs around bars in Glasgow and district, playing a role in local political campaigns. They reformed as The Blues Poets in the early 1990s and in 1993–4 they agreed to take the lead in my 'musical' *One two – hey!* The band took on acting roles as well as performing seven or eight songs. It was just a special thing altogether. Their performance night after night helped keep me sane during the media hullabaloo that followed publication of *How Late It Was, How Late*.

In 1964 The Beatles were everywhere. The first song to make it was 'I Want to Hold Your Hand'. Young Americans walked about in a daze. Within two weeks or less The Beatles' U.K. backlist was rushed onto the market and four more of their singles entered the U.S. top ten.

Not only was I proud, it made sense of my clothes. I had been walking about dressed in Glasgow-style; early mod and strictly working-class. Another couple of years passed before the art-school, cross-class culture appeared and dominated. On the east coast young males were still trying to look like Bobby Darin or Elvis Presley. Where I came from nobody of my generation wanted to look like Elvis – that was your auntie's boyfriend. Teddy Boys and Rockers singing 'I Don't Have a Wooden Heart', you kidding?

In California white youths were more influenced by Archie comics and the Jerry Lewis look; crew cuts and trousers that flapped six inches above the ankles; white socks and thick rubber-soled shoes. They would have been laughed out of Glasgow, Liverpool, Manchester and Newcastle. Thanks to The Beatles I was vindicated, strolling about in my box-cut short jacket, nay vents and cloth-covered buttons; open French-seam trousers, Boston-collar shirt, black socks and chisel-toed shoes.

I still attracted attention, mainly from men around the bus station at 7th and Main. I was naïve but not innocent. Young people of both genders suffer harassment in factories. I coped with it, I think. The situation in Los Angeles was different. My vulnerability lay in the economic. A few years passed till I came upon the work of John Rechy. His *City of Night* was published back in 1963. If I had found a copy then I would have viewed differently the downtown area around Central Library and Pershing Square. Maybe one of these early stories would have been entitled 'Not Raped in California'. The York printer and the Extra-mural class at Glasgow University would have enjoyed it. Hubert Selby's *Last Exit to Brooklyn* was published in 1964 and I had no knowledge of it, nor of the obscenity charges brought against his work in the U.S.A. in 1961, then later in the U.K. in 1968.

The courageous integrity of artists like Selby and Rechy can have an inspirational effect on young writers. Just get on with it, do it honestly, do it properly, tell the fucking truth, just tell it, do it. Whereas, in mainstream English literature young writers are encouraged to find their place in the hierarchy. As an existential experience working-class life was a taboo area and prostitution, like industrial cancer, is a working-class experience, essentially.

While in San José I attended a reading given by a contemporary of mine here in the Bay area. He is a decent writer and a likeable man but his public persona, like many another English novelist, appears modelled on Prince Charles taking a stroll down the charity ward of a Cambridge hospital. During the question/answer session that followed he declared to an audience of maybe 500 people that in his opinion the greatest influence on English novelists of the past thirty years was Philip Larkin.

Honest to god.

But Anglo-American audiences dote on that socio-intellectual embrace. Especially when the individual appears able to cope with the beastlier forms of street life. He reminds them of that English actor who portrays bumbling upper-class characters who stay calmly ironic while dealing with brute reality, even such horrors as having to buy a young black woman to service one orally. They understand such angst and often experience it themselves when making contracts with street people. Even young WASP women share a smile. They empathise with the man buying the woman! The idea of being on your knees in a back alley, staring up at a rich white bastard's penis, seems not to occur.

If only I was a fucking musician, man, why did I have to be a writer, I could just get on with the work as honestly as I could. Music had Eric Burdon, Them, the Stones. We writers had Kingsley Amis and the Angry Young Men.

In the name of fuck.

In those days the clearest statement of my own position came via Steve Marriott and the Small Faces:

Wouldin it be noice,
to get on wiv me nighbirs

and then shout like fuck and bang yer drums and whistle and
stamp yer feet. Instead one is to learn firstly the rudimentaries
that one might come to respect, not simply Standard English
Grammatical Form, but its exigency, how to be a good literary
chap, and know yer place.

Poverty types do exist but it is bad manners to air them
publicly. The bourgeoisie expect beggars to apologise for their
lack of invisibility. Regrettably some beggars do just that. Thus
they seek a pitch nearby a public sewer. Sorry guv, I aint one
of em reds, give me twenty pee and I'll plop dahn the plugole.

Young artists learn how not to deal with life on the street
except at a distance, to subjugate the impulse to create original
art, and look to the fiction-as-sociology mainstream. Stay with
the objective third-party narrative, or that whining first-person
present tense: assimilate that conventional grammar at all costs,
that one might come to describe those curiously shabby, odorous
creatures from the outside, without having to touch, taste or
smell them. Do not attempt to gain entry into their psyches,
you will find that a contradiction in terms; amorphous mobs
and baying multitudes do not 'have' psyches.

Earlier writers tried something different. They knew the lives
of ordinary people and attempted to work from within. It was
not necessary to have experienced everything. But you have to
be sufficiently touched as a human being to address these areas;
you begin from solidarity – a mixture of sympathy and empathy,
a tricky emotion for those in an economically advantaged and
socially superior position. I was ignorant of American writers
like Saroyan, Caldwell, Le Seuer, Ellison. I had no idea of the
existence of stories such as 'Blue Boy', 'The Daring Young Man
on the Flying Trapeze' or 'King of the Bingo Game'?

I read work by writers who touched on it from the outside; in my teens I enjoyed A.J. Cronin and had no knowledge of James Barke or Walter Greenwood. But who tackled poverty and its effects, whether malnutrition or degradation, as an existential experience? In U.K. prose fiction a masterwork such as Knut Hamsun's *Hunger* was a logical absurdity. Fortunately we could learn from European writers in translation.

When I started writing I looked with longing to rock music. It was never to do with being a liberated young male, it was to do with being a liberated young working-class male. The Who's 'My Generation' was exciting but it let the upper classes off the hook once again, it universalised rebellion. You and me brother, the whole world could hold hands and join in. Oh no, here we go, a penny for the black babies. Religion and spirituality and wholefoods and tolerance for one another. Even the richest man in the world will bleed if pricked. Leave the guy alone, he is a suffering soul. Let us read the Beats and rebel against Daddy and his corporate chums. If only they loved one another they could join with Bob Geldof and Bono and become multibillionaire charity heroes. Perhaps then they could dance and let their hair down, use words like 'gig' and 'cool' in context; sniff a line, smoke a joint, listen to Jimi Hendrix, read Ginsberg and not shave on weekends. Thus 'we' might come to halt this beastly systematic brutality being perpetrated by corporate capital on working-class and indigenous communities across the globe. Absafuckinglootely, as they say in Cambridge and Yale.

In 1964 Los Angeles I had no money and no way of getting money. There was no game in town, not that I knew about. Since boyhood me and my pals gambled for money for as long as we had any. Once or twice the cards landed correctly or the horses ran to form. Here in L.A. the local newspapers had racing-form pages. Maybe the locals could make sense of them, I could not. Nor could I find a betting shop. The only money I had was skimmed off the busfares, or given by my father or elder brother. I did not like being in that position. Who does? I was not used to dependency.

So who knows, had I been offered dough by one of the men that hung around the bus station, probably I would have taken it and dealt with the consequences later. I was never completely sure what went on between men anyway. Stories in *An Old Pub Near the Angel* are set in England where I lived from the spring of 1965. The same business option existed there. Two Scottish guys I knew in London had taken the money. One referred to an elderly man who paid him for minor masochistic pleasures. The other said, I would have kicked his arse for ten Woodbine – a cheap brand of no-filter cigarettes; you could buy them in fives. That stuff was incredible to me, and by then I was 21. At 17 I thought anal sex was a metaphor.

In L.A. I just wandered about, along to Grand Central Market; maybe one of the butchers was in need of a delivery boy and I would just happen to be passing and that would be me with a job. My elder brother met my father here on Friday evenings to stock up on food before catching the bus home to Pasadena. By then I was on the road home myself. A hamburger stall on 5th had become my second home. An older man operated the stall, open from 7 a.m. and finished by mid afternoon. He did not know of any jobs for 17-year-olds but offered coffee refills for as long as I stayed.

His hamburgers were magnificent. When he dished one up to me he used to ask, With everything?

He soon stopped asking. Of course with everything, what are ye kidding? Mustard and ketchup, fried onions, chopped jalapeños, pickled gherkins: it was all over my nose and down my neck. I rationed myself to one a fortnight.

I came to realise that he assumed I was Jewish. It was my name. There are more Jewish Kelmans in the U.S.A. than there are Protestant Kelmans in the entire north-east of Scotland, including Macduff. In the 1990s I did a reading in New York City at an Irish club near the Museum of Modern Art. It smelled of money. I read from *How Late It Was, How Late*. A few individuals in the audience hated it, they really hated it, and harrumphed, coughed and spluttered throughout. Afterwards I heard one of the harrumphing elderly men say to his female partner, Kelman is not even a Scottish name, it is Jewish.

The hamburger-stall owner was not put off when I told him I was a Protestant Atheist, as they say in parts of Scotland and Ireland, just embarrassed and apologetic that the subject had arisen. His son was my age and a soccer freak; he tuned in to foreign stations to get results from Europe. For some reason he had latched onto Partick Thistle. I explained to him that there was only one team in Scotland worth bothering about and they played at Pittodrie Park. He never had heard of Graham Leggatt, George Kinnell or Ian Burns, not even Paddy Buckley let alone the legendary 'Gentleman' George Hamilton, my father's hero. When the Dons thrashed Rangers 6–0 in a cup semi-final at Ibrox Park back in the early 1950s, 'Gentleman' George ran amok. As I recall he missed the cup final and Celtic beat us 2–1 before a record 134,000 spectators.

In L.A., football was one of the primary absences in our family's life. My mother was used to us ranting and raving about it but she missed it too. But she was missing everything. With five sons she was accustomed to the absence of female company, but not inured to it. Here she had none at all, and saw nobody. In Glasgow we lived in tenement blocks; six, eight or even twelve families lived up a close, and the next close was a five- to ten-second walk away. It was a community, even if ye hated the neighbours. Here in Pasadena the tied cottage was down at the end of a private lane, nobody except us. A family of animals with striped tails appeared in the evening to stare in the window, watching us watch television.

My father's job at the private gallery in Pasadena deteriorated to the extent that he handed in notice to quit. The owner was looking for cheap labour only, and practised in the arts of obedience. Now she wanted us off the premises immediately. If we stayed even one minute beyond the period of employment, she would have us charged with all sorts of criminal misdemeanours, and each of these minutes would cost us rent.

Our tied cottage was located on the grounds of a large home on Arlington Drive. The owner had a Japanese gardener ages with herself, and an established Japanese garden with plenty shrubbery; bushes and trees and a burn flowing through the middle. There was a wee temple with a shrine where the gardener spent much of his time. My younger brothers, Alan and Philip, ran wild in the garden playing chases, splashing through the burn and sneaking into the temple and making the gardener's life a misery. I climbed up on the roof to keep out the road, reading and sunbathing. My mother spent most of her time in the tied cottage, doing the domestic work and dreaming of Scotland. The mindset we entered into reminds me of that opening in the Cassavetes movie *Gloria*. The accountant father has cooked the books of his employers, a team of mafioso. It is useless to run. His wife has bouts of rage, then lapses into lethargy, like her mother and daughter, just staring at him occasionally, as they wait for the executioner. It is a brilliant scene.

One of my father's ex co-workers was our saviour, a young Puerto Rican picture-framer by the name of Mario. My father had been free with his skills to the other workers. Now Mario was quick to offer his support. They hatched a plot a week or so later. In Glasgow we call it 'doing a moonlight'. Mario had a rusty old banger, wings falling to bits, exhaust system knackered. They stuffed everybody in, bags and suitcases, the lot, and we hightailed it out of town, straight onto Pasadena Freeway, Mario's car rattling and shaking the whole way south to an apartment in Hawthorne, south L.A. This was more like it.

Hawthorne is next door to Watts where much racist violence hit the street in 1965. Around 15,000 National Guard troops were sent in to show the black American community who was boss. On any bus into town I sat at the back because I was a smoker. Only blacks sat there, whites went to the front. Sometimes the back of the bus was crowded and only a few seats being used in the white section. None of the whites gave me a row, they just kind of looked, as did the blacks, but nothing more than that. Not even a vague frown, that I recall. Perhaps the clothes I wore advertised my foreign origins. What happened to other colours or ethnicities, I do not know, I do not know.

Walking about in L.A. was no different from walking through the foreign neighbourhoods of Drumchapel: not for youths. This pressure is known to almost every full-sighted urban male that breathes, every day of our lives. Who will step out the way first? After an entire day tramping the streets, one wearies of the constant decision-making, and the longer it goes on the more complex the judgment. I start making *a priori* decisions: it does not matter the male, for every second one I shall step out of the road. For every third male over the age of 70 I shall keep my ground and stick out my elbows.

Then you start playing games: I think I will step out the road of this cunt and see if he smiles, if he smiles I will batter him across the fucking skull. By the end of the evening ye weary of everything and just step out everybody's way. Then ye start making a virtue out of it. After you!

No, after you.

Please, take my ground.

No, you take my ground.

Take my ground ya bastard.

Fuck you man, fucking fag bastard.

Wait a minute you I am from Scotland we always look at guys, nay ambiguity intended.

In California they have detox macho units where males learn how to step out of the other man's path. It is a rich, rewarding field of study, all the more so for its increasing complexity. Just when you think you have mastered the basics ye land on yer back. I was trudging along a quiet, tree-lined street at dusk. Sixty yards away a guy approached. We were heading along the same track of the same path. Aw naw.

Nobody else was in sight. I walked on, less steadily. From many yards off I decided to step sideways. I just made the decision. I just thought I cannot be bothered with this. Even so, I did the manoeuvre from far off, so it would seem like a natural, absent-minded veer, rather than me being forced out by him and his damn presence. He just kept coming, he just kept on. I did not care. Now I saw he was black, a sturdy-looking guy, still not slowing, but he knew I was coming. When we passed he said, God bless you brother.


My father had a start in one of the picture-framers on La Cienega Boulevard. Quite a few galleries and linked businesses were there. Some still are. I passed through L.A. in the late 1990s and checked to see. My father much preferred this job; Puerto Rican and Central American workmates, a lively atmosphere. But the money was poor and the work repetitive; almost no gilding, let alone picture restoring. The apartment was costly and with seven of us there my mother was working miracles. He could not afford to buy a car. He still had not acquired his driver's licence. These things take ages. It was difficult getting a day off work, then when he did it was problematic with buses, and they took so long to get anyplace, and you got sick of not being understood, repeating the same questions time and time again.

Though wearying of it myself I still went on the tramp once or twice. Word arrived about a Scottish fast-food joint. My brother had spotted it from the bus. It was miles away but worth a shot. Maybe if I threw myself on their mercy, in a guid Scotch tongue, they would give me a start. I got the busfare and next morning set out. I got off the bus too early and had to continue on foot. Then I found the place, it was a proper Scottish name – McDonald's. Two white American lassies were serving. They noticed me. It became a male v. female interlude. I was enjoying it. I hung about by the counter awaiting an opportunity to chat, all too aware that my only line was, Any jobs?

I gave up and went hame. About my last throw of the dice came via an advertisement in a newspaper. A big soccer day was scheduled one Saturday. Teams of players of different nationalities were involved. There was bound to be a Scottish contingent. Maybe I could make a connection. Secretly, I still dreamt about making the grade as a player. There were a few semi-pro teams in the Los Angeles area. Some junior and ex-senior Scottish players had gone out, in the twilight of their years. I was never anywhere near that standard but this was America, could they even tell the difference? At least I was young. I decided to have a go. The one genuinely great Scottish player to have made L.A. his base was before my time but his name was still known and my father had seen him play; the Scottish international and ex-Dundee inside-forward Billy Steel.

If a U.S. team signed you they ensured you had a day job. Even if I was not good enough to play maybe somebody would know about a day job. Off I went. A bus into downtown then another one out. Miles away as usual. In area, Los Angeles was the biggest city in the world, in those days something like 35 miles wide. When I reached the football ground, to my dismay, the entrance fee alone would swallow up every cent of busfare I had left. I would be stranded, and the walk home was as bad as the Pasadena marathon.

Three games were to be played consecutively. Okay, it was good value. I agreed with the guy on the turnstile. But I only needed to see the one featuring the Scottish players. I argued it out but to no avail: full entrance fee or nothing. Watch the football or get a bus home. No contest. My whole world depended on it. In the stadium I strolled to one of the empty seats. There was a German team, an Italian team, a Mexican team, a British team and a couple from Central America. Where were the Scottish boys? Maybe I missed them.

At the final whistle of the final game I wandered towards the exit, postponing the reality of the long hike home. Then there on the ground, was a crumpled but complete copy of the Saturday 'Pink' *Times*!

In the old days the proprietors of the Glasgow *Evening Times* published a late edition on a Saturday afternoon that gave all the sports results. They used pink newspaper to distinguish it from the boring early editions. The newspaper I found was a fortnight old but it induced a spring in my step and every mile or so I was stopping to read extraordinary snippets of news. Brechin City 0–0 Alloa Athletic, Maryhill Juniors 7–1 Pollok. Was I dreaming?

And then the racing news. The Grand National approached! My god. Dunky Keith rode two winners for Walter Nightingall at Kempton Park. I might have known. They'd always done well at Kempton. And had Arkle beaten Mill House for the Gold Cup? And what about the two- and four-dog combination at the White City? Or the three- and five-dogs at Shawfield. I would have kicked myself if that forecast had entered a winning run.

What about the mighty Dons? Had maestro Charlie Cooke left Dundee yet? Oh man! And how was Jim Baxter playing?

Was Denis Law in Torino? All this and more. I was gloating in anticipation of the response my 'Pink' *Times* would get from my father and brothers. Maybe I could charge them a dollar for every result I told them. All of these hot topics from 6,000 miles away.

Except the road went on forever and I was still trudging and my fucking feet man, these shoes I had, fucking chisel-toed winkle-picking bastards or some such nonsense, where had I bought them? Gordon's Shoe Shop in Partick, if I remember rightly, they were fucking killing me and I still had not reached the downtown area.

A couple of months on and my parents called it quits. My mother had never enjoyed the experience and my father just worked, slept, ate and travelled on buses. In many ways it was a typical immigrant experience. For my parents it was a case of cutting the losses, getting home as soon as possible. At least we had a country to go to. But they did not have enough money for everybody's fares. My elder brother decided he could stay, look after himself and our younger brother Alan who was 15 years old and attending school. He would save to pay Alan's flight home. It was a burden for a 21-year-old but he managed it fine. Alan returned home a few months later, but Ronnie stayed and has been there ever since, now with his wife and four grown-up children.

I had no option but to return to Scotland. The decision was a family one. I was doing nothing anyway. Back in Glasgow I could work and contribute to the family purse. There was the possibility of returning to the States later.

The printer's factory over in Partick could not take me back. The firm was agreeable but it was a union shop; I had severed my apprenticeship and that was that. But really, I had no complaints. The S.O.G.A.T. secretary had warned me months ago.

I stayed with my grandparents in Govan, my mother's parents, and got a job on the line at the Cooperative shoe factory in Shieldhall, earning a man's wage on piecework. Then a letter arrived from Pasadena weeks after my eighteenth birthday. The printers on Colorado Boulevard were holding the job open for me. I did consider it but decided against.

This was the period when I knew I was never going to be a painter. I still fancied the art business. I had discovered, perhaps through my father, that a college existed in Europe that specialised in a course for art dealers. I had discussed it with my elder brother for a time, and my father. If I completed the course in art dealing, Ronnie would save dough in the States and send money home, and I could make use of that to buy and sell art. By this time he was in the U.S. Army. We were serious about it. But life was getting on top of me at that time and I needed away.

The immigrant experience left an obvious mark on our family, as it does on every immigrant family. We were never together again as a unit. My younger brother Alan found life unsettling. In 1971 he crossed to New York City to be best man at our brother Ronnie's wedding. He did not come home for eight years; he travelled south to work for a time in the Pennsylvania hills, then Florida, Texas, Death Valley, Nevada and other places in between. He has his own stories. Before then, in Glasgow, when he turned 16 he discovered the music clubs in the city: the Electric Garden, the Lindella Club, Bruce's Cave and the rest. He worked on the door at the Picasso Club, and occasionally borrowed 45 RPM EPs from the D.J. The first time I heard the name James Brown was from Alan. He was clutching that very early EP, *Papa's Got a Brand New Bag*, from 1965.

My head was not in music so much. I had discovered other

clubs around Glasgow, with names like the Raven, the Hanover, the Coronet, the Starlight Rooms, the Blue Dolphin, the 44 Club, the Establishment, the Cigar Club, the White Elephant and the New Businessman's Club. The latter was known locally as 'the Busy', a play on words; the police also were known locally as 'the busies'. I was 18 at that time.

These were gambling clubs of one kind or another; *chemin-de-fer* – chemmy – the most popular game; and five-card stud poker for afters, for those left with money. I preferred the atmosphere in gambling clubs but it was a tougher world than that of Damon Runyon, though I was fond of 'Big Nig' and 'The Lemondrop Kid'. The guy on the door on these clubs stared at ye, looked left and right, then nodded ye in. Occasionally I brought along guests, my pals. They were very impressed. I whispered, Mind now, ye have to be quiet, and for fuck sake do not chat up the lasses, they are all on the game.

One night I returned to a club from a greyhound track with money burning its way through both trouser pockets. People were around but it was quiet, a man had been stabbed to death at the door. Guys were coming in to play cards and saying, That's bad news about the bloke on the door ... Then they coughed quietly, So, what, is there nay cards later on or what?

In another club there was a £1,500 bank for afternoon sessions at faro. I was a busconductor out at Gavinburn Depot, Old Kilpatrick. One day I had a 'spare' duty. But it was payday. Everybody goes to work on payday. I was hanging about the garage doing nothing. We could not even watch television in the garage bothy. One of the conductresses had switched it on but nothing happened. Eventually we looked round the back of it to check the electrics. There was nothing there. It was a shell. Some dirty bastard stole the tube and all the inner workings. That was typical at Gavinburn Depot – the garage was fucking notorious; after forty years I still remember the name of the garage superintendent – wee Dunbar!

To pass the time I skipped down to the village bookie and bet a double at Cheltenham; Ken Oliver's brilliant novice, Arctic Sunset, and Jimmy Scot, trained by Fulke Walwyn. They fucking bolted home. I lifted the dough and went back to the Depot, but couldnay stand it, signed off sick and went straight to the Hanover club for a game of faro. The guy on the door looked at me. I was still in the busconductor uniform. Jesus Christ, son, he said.

When I walked into the card room there was guffaws: Aw look, the buses is here.

The gambling clubs in *A Chancer* are based on those named above. And the snooker hall Tammas frequents is the old Imperial, Mitchell Street. He lives with his sister and brother-in-law on the Anderston side of St Vincent Street, prior to the M8 upheaval and the demolition of the tenements from Elliot Street.

But oh that gambling. Life is a complication. I forgot about art dealing in Paris, card dealing in Glasgow, I needed away, fast. I went to Manchester with a pal, Colin Hendry from Partick who died a few years ago. His elder brother Ian was a plumber to trade; he died some years before Colin. We played football and cards together, gin rummy for the entire trip down by train. Colin could lose patience. When our train pulled into Victoria Station, Manchester that Friday afternoon in the spring of 1965 I had to make a confession: Colin, I said, I only have twelve and a tanner (63 pence in new money).

Aw for fucksake Jimmy, how did ye no tell me?

Because ye wouldnay have come.

Aye, ye are fucking right I wouldnay.

We bought two bags of chips and went to find the nearest Department of Social Security.

Eventually we got a start at a Salford copper mill producing coils of copper wire. We left the down-and-outs' hostel, found a room at a place doing dinner, bed and breakfast. Huge meals.

It was heavy, difficult work, semi-skilled. For Colin it was temporary; I was enquiring about pension schemes. A week into the job and they tried us on a section where we had to grab white-hot lengths of copper bar with a pair of extreme clamps. We had thick gloves to protect our hands. Often the material had worn away; you had to be careful the clamps did not connect with your skin. The first time Colin was given the clamps, he managed to get them round the white-hot copper bar but was unable to connect in a move, thus he took the full weight of the copper length, could not hold it, it rolled off the bogey onto the floor. Being a decent football player Colin did the instinctive thing, he 'trapped' the white-hot bar, and his shoe burst into flames. He threw his clamps to one side, threw me a look and off he went. The gaffer came to find out the problem. Colin threw him a look as well, and continued walking, shoe smouldering. A few days later he got a proper job as an electrician. He was 21 and had only finished his apprenticeship weeks previously. I used that incident in a story.

A while later I lifted my insurance cards and P45, collected the week's lying time, and went home for a holiday. I had some dirty laundry my mother insisted on washing. They were still living in a two-room flat down a dunny in Gibson Street, my mother and father in the kitchen, the four of us in two double beds. I stayed in my Govan grannie's some of the time. My mother showed me the dirty-washing water left by my jeans and working clothes. It was full of a thick green dye. Aye, right enough, I remembered also when ye smoked a fag it always tasted sweet, and every hour or so the gaffer told ye to swallow some green solution that tasted like concentrated lime.

I planned to return to England. I took a job on the buses to save enough money for the fare and the settling-in period. Thoughts of industrial disease or injury were not to the fore; I returned to the same factory.

One time I was showing a new guy how we coiled the copper wire. This was the end of the wire-making process. The wire would have been between a half and three quarters of an inch in diameter. I do not know what length it was, maybe 50 or 60 yards. The big coiling machine was shaped like a ship's steering wheel. Once the wire coiled onto it one man got a pair of heavy-duty clamps and gripped the end of the wire to keep it secure, otherwise the coil sprung. He kept one foot on the bottom of the wheel to stop it spinning. The man needs to use his wrist and arm muscles, at the same time concentrate on gripping the end. At this stage the wire is not yet trained into its coil, and is very powerful, fighting to spring. If it does the wire is ruined, no longer malleable and cannot be recoiled. Of course that spring is also dangerous, its whiplash is unpredictable.

While the one man grips tightly the end of the wire his mate has another pair of clamps which he uses to twist the wire some ten inches or so from the end. He inserts this twisted end into the coil so that it cannot spring. The first man continues gripping the end until certain that his mate has made the twist and can take the strain.

I was showing the new guy how this was to be done when he lost concentration, and thus control, and the coil sprung, the end lashed me across the cheek and eye. It was my cheekbone saved me from losing the eye. My face was cut open across there and my eyebrow. The new man was crestfallen. Nay fucking wonder. I did not have much sympathy for him. He was a strong cunt as well, it was his concentration that faltered.

I sat in the doctor's waiting room holding a rag to my eye to stop it landing on the floor. In this factory they used dropped eyes as ball bearings. I was offered a job in the boiler room after that; twelve-hour shifts, alternate nightshift, dayshift. They also had a snooker table in their welfare club. And a works football team that played on grass pitches. And down the road was Salford Greyhound Track, with a casino at the first bend.

I was still there when Germany were denied the World Cup. Denis Law spent the afternoon playing golf; we went for a game of snooker. A guy called Charlie had moved into the rooming house. He wanted to play on a regular basis and, next to myself, was the finest loser I ever met. I made a story out of it, 'Charlie'.

Next time in Manchester four friends came along, one has been a friend since boyhood, Ian Lithgow, another great reader. Two of us got a start in a Trafford Park factory with the cleanest working conditions I ever encountered. This was a huge asbestos company.

Our workmates in the asbestos plant were mainly Jamaicans, Poles, Ukrainians and Hungarians. I learned not to assume a person's politics because of their background. You never knew people's lives, what their families had experienced. They were generous men and shared their grub and tobacco, but discussions could veer off track. The East Europeans did not say much in English, just looked and smiled. An older Hungarian was respected by the other men. He spoke better English and had a certain mildness of manner, indicating one used to authority. Ian Lithgow worked with him. On one occasion he was close to losing his temper with me over politics. I had referred to communism in a positive way. It was my own naïvety. I wanted to know why they were here. I wanted to talk about life in a 'socialist country'.

Of course they had not come from any socialist country, they had come from Stalin's brand of so-called communism. I was 19 and probably had not connected that there was a link between a real live Hungarian person and the actual events that had occurred ten years earlier in Hungary. His and Ian's job was weighing out the white asbestos fibre and cement in tubs. Ian had red hair. Half an hour into the shift and the pair were like snowmen, fibre clinging to their eyebrows, in their ears and up their nose.

The wee guy who taught me my job was Polish and spoke no English. He shared everything. Rye bread and thick salami, hot sweet tea and roll-ups thicker than a cigar, and loaned me dough if I was skint. He was very patient, and showed me how not to clean the chute and asbestos mixer by hand. But he occasionally did it himself and if he caught me looking just grinned and shrugged, cigarette dowt hanging from his mouth. Eventually I took over the mixing operation at that machine, and he moved to a different shift.

The biggest man on the floor was a Ukrainian who moved with the slow precision of a weightlifter. He rarely spoke but laughed a lot. In Anglo-American litrachuhh the narrator would describe him as 'a hulking brute', unless the upper-class hero was not intimidated by his physicality in which case he would be described as 'a great oaf' or 'a lumbering jackass', and be felled by the hero 'with one mighty swoop to the jaw'. My grannie would have called him 'a big handsome man'.

The best-dressed guy on the floor was a Jamaican whose name I think was Danny. He worked directly beneath me on the spreading table. The asbestos and cement came from Ian Lithgow to me. I mixed a concrete that consisted of a tub of asbestos fibre and half a tub of cement, and a certain amount of water. Then I dumped it down a chute. On the level below me the 'spreader', the Jamaican, opened the trapdoor, and let the mix pour out. He spread it then rolled it into asbestos sheets. Each month we did a batch of blue asbestos, the deadliest fibre. When I was learning I erred and forgot to put in the cement element of the composition. Danny released the chute trapdoor and out splashed a tidal wave of asbestos paste. I had forgotten to put in the solidifier. I looked over the rail to apologise. He was covered in stuff, wiping it out his eyes and mouth. The spreading job was supposed to be one of the cleaner ones, that was how he could wear decent clothes doing it. It was my first experience with the less familiar aspects of Jamaican English, beginning with a paean to the old ska song 'Judge Dread in Court', with slightly different lyrics to Prince Buster; I will kill you I will torture you I will fucking lynch you ras clat fuck blood scotch twat fucker blaaad claat.

And the wee Polish guy tugging at my elbow, conveying that I should not approach him for a couple of days, as if I had intended any such thing. In Manchester they all call you a twat. They all called *me* a twat anyway. A few years later I discovered twat did not mean 'silly fool', it meant 'vagina'. Ach well.

It was a tricky job but paid good money and sometimes you could work double shifts. If me and Ian had done the dough and were extra hungry we stole dry bread from the canteen bins out in the deserted parking lot, spread on layers of asbestos, applied a little brown sauce with the blue and white. What a tasty mouthful. This asbestos company operated an Employees' Suggestions box throughout the world. In view of mounting litigation costs new uses for asbestos fibre were especially welcome. I tipped them the one about sandwiches and they now export them to service station fast-food outlets on foreign shores. Ian and myself are in touch about twice a year; we have an interest in each other's symptoms, and wonder if we are the last of that batch of factory hands.

On a few Saturdays, with the other three guys that came with us, we went to Old Trafford to watch United; Law, Best and Charlton, Paddy Crerand. When Denis scored the fans sang:

> The King Has Scored Again
> The King Has Scored Again
> eee aye addio
> The King Has Scored Again

My heart beat loudly. We also went to Maine Road to watch the City and Colin Bell, Johnny Crossan, Mike Summerbee.

I watched many strange games in Manchester. In one of them Man City destroyed Tottenham Hotspur for 88 minutes. But they did not have Jimmy Greaves and Alan Gilzean. Two break-aways, two flicked headers, two goals. Tottenham won 2–0. The pair of them walked off the field chortling, pair of baldy bastards. But Alan Gilzean, what a fucking player! But so was Greaves, one has to confess.

My loyalties were split one day at Old Trafford. Jim Baxter had signed for Sunderland and the team was full of Scottish players. They had a great team but unfortunately did little on the park to show it. Baxter had thickened, and was not the player of old, but still capable of plenty. He played a few years on from then.

Several months before that game in 1964, when I was in Glasgow, a horrible tragedy had occurred. John White, a Scottish internationalist, was killed by lightning while playing a round of golf. White was a highly regarded inside right, known as 'the ghost', a member of the Tottenham Hotspur team of the early 1960s. For myself, and thousands of other boys, it was always Law and Baxter, but John White was a hero too.

Davie Mackay was in that same Spurs team. Nobody would have accused him of 'swashbuckling', he would have lifted ye up by the jersey and stared ye right in the eye, even if ye were Billy Bremner. Men prefer that, but boys like the 'swashbuck-lers'. Scottish sports journalists describe football-artists in these terms, unless they are wee guys like Jimmy Johnstone, a 'buzzbomb bundle of tireless energy'. In addition to Baxter and Law my own heroes were Lester Piggott and the Cincinnati Kid.

Jim Baxter was still with Rangers at the time of John White's funeral. He called into the gents' outfitters, Jackson the Tailor, at 76 Union Street with a pair of old black trousers. Downstairs he came to the alterations section in the basement and inter-rupted a period of quiet. I was working in Jackson the Tailor for a couple of months. It was mid morning. Me and the old guy who worked down there were reading the *Sporting Life* and discussing race form in a side room. We heard the footsteps coming down and my older mate went to serve the customer. It was his turn, we took turn about with customers. I sat on with the *Sporting Life*. But to my horror I saw it was Jim Baxter, in his shirtsleeves. Nobody came into a tailor shop in their shirtsleeves, not in them days boy, no sir.

The older guy was laughing across at me, he knew I was a fan. Then he relented and called me over to continue the job. Baxter needed the alteration in a rush. It was the only pair of black trousers he had. He never bought stuff 'off the peg', it was always made-to-measure. But there was no time to get a new pair made, this was a rush job, he was flying down for John White's funeral and needed them immediately. The trousers had to be altered, the trousers taken in or let out or something. He was still quite skinny in those days. I listened and noted everything. A rush job, immediately, John White's funeral, a rush job. Then he was off up the stairs, whistling a cheery wee tune to himself. I heard his footsteps dying away. Then I had to dash through to the alterations room and see the crabbit auld cunt that did the tailoring alterations. Robert, I said, this is a rush job, immediately and it is just, it is a rush job, honest.

What ye mumbling about, rush job, I do not give a fuck if it is a rush job.

Aye but it is Jim Baxter.

I do not give a fuck if it is – who?

Jim Baxter.

I do not give a fuck if it is Jim Baxter, the job will take a fucking week.

But Robert, it is for John White's funeral.

I do not give a rat's fucking tadger if it is the fucking Queen's fucking – who?

John White.

You must think I am stupit. Here, give me them.

Thanks Robert.

Shut the fucking door on yer way out.

The trousers were altered, pressed, packed and ready to go, on schedule. And he had done the actual repair job. Usually he just slapped the trousers three times with his heaviest iron and muttered, That will do the cunt. Then he flung the trousers or jacket at ye, Give that peg for two days.

'Peg for two days' meant ye folded the trousers or jacket on a hanger and hung it up for two days. When the customer came in for his new suit complete with alterations ye had to pretend it was all done and hope the guy would not ask to try it on again. Once ye had him out the door ye knew he would wear the unaltered trousers and just fit his way into them, or else get his wife or his maw to do the job.

But Robert did the genuine alteration on this occasion. Everybody knew about Baxter's funeral trousers and was waiting for his return. But I planked the trousers so nobody could steal the job off me. That was what the salesmen did to one another when a personality came in the shop, especially football players, and a few football players did come in. Everybody rushed to serve them. Sometimes the manager himself took the job, hoping he would wind up with an order for eleven blazers and eleven pairs of flannels.

I couldnay bear the thought of missing Baxter. I had been

a fan since his Raith Rovers days, way before his £17,500 transfer to Rangers. My Uncle Lewie stayed in Kirkcaldy and through there they all knew about Baxter from his days as a Junior.

So what if I missed serving him! What if I was in the smoke-room for a quick puff? What if I skipped out to the betting shop? Or if I went round to the Imperial Billiards Parlour where I usually spent my lunch break watching the money games? A couple of the salesmen came too, there were always huge queues and no time to play. But on this occasion I would not have wasted time on any such nonsense. I sat at the counter and waited. In case of emergencies I planked the trousers so nobody could find them. They would have to come and find me first.

Unfortunately I had to charge Jim Baxter 10/6 (53 pence) for the alteration to his black trousers. Old Robert was one of these ancient codgers you get in the tailoring business. They glower at ye over the top of their specs, and insist on petty detail. I do not care who he is, away out there and get the ten and a tanner!

In those days football players still travelled on public trans-port. In the shop doorway of Jackson the Tailor a few Rangers players met in the morning. There was a bus stop outside the doorway. The players were going to Ibrox. They came in from the east coast to Central Station, and crossed the road to wait for a 15 bus along Paisley Road West. Baxter was not one of them. He was not a 'buses' kind of footballer. When he left Rangers he went to play for Sunderland. I was at Old Trafford when he came with his new Sunderland teammates.

It was one of those strange games that occur from time to time. After a full 90 minutes' play the final whistle blows, and the fans walk hesitantly to the exits. Gradually their foreheads start wrinkling, they start looking at one another, some scratching their heads, the puzzled frowns begin. The boys are taking notes, waiting to see what they should think. Then one of the younger men says suddenly, What the fuck was that about?

And another one nods. That must have been one of the weirdest games I have ever seen.

Weird! says a grizzled 60-year-old, I have never seen a game like that in my entire fucking puff.

Aye but what happened? says a younger man.

Fucked if I know!

Then a burly man with the look of a retired boxer strides past, shoulders barging, shaking his head, speechless, just fucking speechless. They continue homeward.

At Old Trafford that day the English fans were not too bothered about Baxter one way or another. But many Scotsmen, as well as Irishmen, attended the games at Old Trafford and they were anticipating something special. Baxter wore the number 10 jersey and played inside-left. He was not outstanding but he played well. I thought it was a great game, and very even. Yet it was one of these peculiar spectacles where you want to discuss important pointers, but cannot find the words. United won 5–1. Of course they did. I know they did. But it was still an even game. How come?

Others among the Sunderland Scottish contingent included a fine ex-Aberdeen winger, George Mulhall, also cousins George Herd and Alec Herd. There was a third Herd on the pitch that day, another Scottish player. Man U had just signed Davie Herd from Arsenal – I think for £45,000 – a right-winger. United fans were perplexed by the signing. He was nothing at all like George Best. He looked more like 'big Yogi', John Hughes of Celtic, but without the nifty footwork. This was the day Davie Herd scored four goals.

On their way out the ground the Man U supporters were still unconvinced, not willing to concede the point. One of them delivered the classic cliché: Fucking twat, he only kicked the ball four times.

From the tail end of 1966 through to 1969 I lived and worked mostly in London, until Marie and I married in early November. I had been writing for several months and completed a couple of stories from *An Old Pub Near the Angel*. We had met the previous March, appropriately enough on St David's Day, her being Welsh. She was working as a shorthand typist. I sold suits on Oxford Street, laboured on a building site down Harley Street, then a building site at the Barbican, plus spells in other jobs. In one of them it coincided we worked in the same place, the Royal Free Hospital, where she had reported from her agency. We were living together but pretended not to know each other.

A busdriver I knew from Glasgow was living in Bracknell, outside of London. He and his wife, Dorothy, had invited me to come and stay the night. I had just met Marie and invited her to come with me. She refused on the grounds of ulterior motivation. But I was just showing off, acting like a cool guy with friends in out-of-the-way places. If I arrived in Bracknell with Marie by my side maybe they would recognise the striking similarity of the image we presented to that early album cover of Bob Dylan and his girlfriend, her on his elbow, photographed in Manhattan.

But maybe not. Chris Harvey was not easily impressed, not then, not now. Back in Glasgow he had been over 21 so could drive buses. I was under 21 so I could not, I was the damn conductor, then serving my third or fourth sentence. Harvey gave me no peace, insisting on the merits of Sartre, in opposition to Camus, of Mann as opposed to Kafka, van Gogh rather than Gauguin, Russell against Wittgenstein; he saw merit in Thomas Hardy and D.H. Lawrence, and thought *The Go Between* one of the finest novels ever written. I disagreed with everything he said, never having read the damn books, and no wonder. I was unwilling to consider these possibilities, strictly on a point of logic. But Chris is not the model for the character Willie Reilly, busdriving sparring partner of the central character in *The Busconductor Hines*. For one thing he is English and for another the bastard knew too much, even at 21.

For my and Marie's wedding night party we had four singles: 'Lazy Sunday', The Small Faces; 'Lay Lady Lay', Bob Dylan; 'I Heard It through the Grapevine', Marvin Gaye; and a nice one by Billy Preston whose title I cannot remember.

A friend in North London, Gavin Allison, gave us the use of the front room in his flat so we could have a party. Gavin was another good reader and we bumped heads frequently, usually on the subject of James Jones, his favourite author.

Marie was pregnant and had to stop work late November. Accommodation in London was not easy to find, not on a labourer's wage, with a baby on the way. We tramped around looking. Racist stuff still applied. Blacks and Irish were unwelcome, Scots had it easier, but babies were out the question unless one was loaded with dosh. Swansea or Glasgow became the option. We decided on Glasgow. By this time my father was back self-employed and had found that decent wee workshop in Garriochmill Road. He 'spoke' for us with the factor, laid down some key money as a wedding present, and we rented the room and kitchen up on the second floor.

Our next-door neighbours were an elderly couple by the name of Bradford. Mr Bradford came from the North of Ireland. He looked and dressed like a proper businessman in the three-piece suit and soft hat. His business was a private lending library in a wee shop across the street: the Garriochmill Library. He charged threepence to borrow a book.

He had just retired when we came to stay there but his house was full of old library books, most of which were written by

Lloyd C. Douglas and Edgar Burroughs, but included a few by John Steinbeck, Erskine Caldwell, Walter Greenwood and A.J. Cronin. I could borrow any I wanted and he always enjoyed a chat.

After he died his widow let me take what I wanted. I have to confess there were not too many I did want, but a few I still have. The circumstances surrounding his death were sad. Mrs Bradford had been away staying with relatives and he was alone. We had not seen him for a few days. Myself and Frank McGoohan, the upstairs neighbour, were banging on his door. Then we forced it in. He took one side of the flat and I the other. I found him dead, in the act of getting into his bed. He had the alarm clock in one hand and must have been setting the alarm, and just sank back when the heart attack hit. I stood there looking. Frank came ben to tell me that a taxi had just drawn up on the street and Mrs Bradford was getting out. We had to move quickly, meet her on the stair, take her into my house.

This part of North Woodside was full of life forty years ago; small businesses by the score. Butchers, bakers, carpentry shops, chemists, drapers and domestic repair shops; secondhand book-shops, launderettes, chip shops, newsagents and dairies; a sweetie shop, a crockery shop, secondhand furniture stores; many pubs, bookies, pawn shops, fish shops and licensed grocers: all within five minutes from the foot of my close, and from South Woodside Road to St Clair Street, taking in Henderson Street, Mount Street, Carrickarden Street and Dick Street. We did not need Great Western Road or Maryhill Road. I am not even including Raeberry Street in this, although I recall the Shakespeare Bar served three-course lunches for 2/6 around 1972. Nah, my memory is surely defective on that one.

When my family returned from the States things were tough

and my mother needed to go out to work. But doing what? She began the long haul to become a teacher. She secured the necessary Highers at day school then entered Teacher Training College. Napiershall Street Primary School was a short walk from my close. My mother taught there from the late 1960s for a period of six or seven years. It was her first job since 1942. My elder daughter Laura was one of her pupils for a year. She was under instructions never to greet her in the playground and never to say 'grannie' in the classroom. She was allowed to give secret smiles.

I was good friends with Frank McGoohan, my upstairs neighbour. He was divorced, a few years older than me, and lived alone. The last couple of days before payday he was always skint but rarely accepted Marie's offer to come in for his tea. He was another reader, and was writing a novel based on his conscription days with the military. After Marie he was the next person to see my stuff. We passed our writings to each other. Frank was fond of English poetry, Keats and Shelley. He could not thole some of my spellings in 'Nice to be Nice'. My rendition of 'Wedinsday' just fucking annoyed him. We agreed that 'Wensday' was more exact. But I argued that 'nsday' was just a glottal stop and I had to reject it. The central character in 'Nice to be Nice' is narrating a story from his recent life but assumes an audience and shifts his pronunciation accordingly: he resists glottal stops.

After a few pints discussing all that in the Gowdoc Bar with Frank, the Creative Writing class at Glasgow University Extramural Department was a doddle.

The possibility of revising my early stories of course has occurred to me. I find it impossible. The author of *An Old Pub Near the Angel* is in his early twenties and with his characters right at the heart of the experience; a smoke, a meal, sex, a beer, the next bet, a relationship. At the same time he – the author – was trying to be a proper parent and husband, helping prepare the bottle, doing a feed, changing the nappy, telling a bedtime story.

I was happy doing all that. I enjoyed it very much. I loved seeing my daughters grow up. Before publication of the book I became friends with Tom Leonard who had two sons. We had disagreements but shared an outlook that included a way to conduct yourself as artist, husband and parent. None of that writer-as-adolescent shite: acknowledge the responsibilities and try to cope. I think we further agreed that if it was impossible to be both artist and father there was something wrong with art. I doubt if we would share that opinion nowadays.

The writing crowded in. I was chewing the nails until I could get my work out on the kitchen table, or spread on the carpet, to sort through the pages. Reading yesterday's first draft was always an exciting experience. The lack of working time was a continual source of stress, as it still is. The frustration worms its way through rage and bitterness, and can lead to breakdown, and silence. I returned to the lives, as well as the works, of writers and artists, particularly Franz Kafka. He too appreciated the early novels of Knut Hamsun.

I saw it as the fundamental and shaping struggle in each, the need to do your work in the face of the socio-economic reality. There was no place in society for your work, as with Cézanne, van Gogh and the rest. Your only requirement was to do *their* work. Who the fuck were they? These bastards. Who wants to do their work? Let them do it themselves, tell them to go and fuck.

Young writers seek bonds of solidarity with older generations; we look for things in common. If a writer comes to mean something to us we want to discover affinities. How did they live their life? What hardships did they endure to pursue their art? How long did it take them to write a story? Kafka did

*The Metamorphosis* in a couple of nights. Oh, I don't believe it, no, no, for godsake, no.

Yes. Now pick yourself up, brush yourself down. Van Gogh did not even begin until he was 28. And look at Tolstoy, a hero at 22, a hero at 72. Phew.

The biographies I read back in my teens proved worthwhile in context. I have been an atheist since 12 so I do not know where the *Lives of the Saints* lead ye, but the lives of the artists lead you to other artists, philosophers and other thinkers. Cézanne's life led me to Émile Zola; then van Gogh's letters, Turgenev's essaying; through Kafka's journals you go everywhere.

Yet I still found difficulty in connecting with writers who had no reason to worry about money and job security. I was prejudiced against Turgenev for years, until it dawned on me how influenced I had been by Dostoevski's judgment, arrived at through a suicidal gambling habit. I would have sat down for a game of poker with Dostoevski but knew I would not have enjoyed it. I aye imagined him jumping up from the table and flinging a cape round his shoulders, This is too slow, too slow! and marching out into the night.

When I read Mary Gray Hughes' first collection, *The Thousand Springs* (Puckerbrush Press, 1971), I was very taken with the title story. It is set back in time and takes the form of the diary of a young woman surviving in desperate circumstances. She is the wife of a smallholder barely eking out a living from the land, just about coping with running the home. Her son is gravely ill, perhaps close to death. And the woman is trying also to be a writer, a writer who loves literature, who loves other writers. She is fighting for her own time and space, that point in the evening when the chores are done and she manages a clear 15 minutes. That is what she can count on: 15 minutes. During that brief period she will go at it and take from it what she can. At the end of the story we discover that the young woman did not 'become' a writer, but her son did.

I think of another literary hero, Agnes Owens. What if Agnes had been 'granted' a proper chance to write when she was fighting to rear her family? As if it was not enough of a burden raising eight children, she spent years going out to work in whatever capacity, servant to the middle classes, clearing up their domestic mess. When she saw the squeak of a chance she grabbed it and produced those great stories that we know. How much more could it have been?

That part of her life she holds in common with Tillie Olsen who was writing in her teens then had to shut down in order to rear a family. And 'shut down' may give a sense of what happens; it is a part of your being that closes, like entering 'sleep' mode on a computer, if you are lucky, otherwise it is forever. Tillie Olsen returned to her art from around the age of 40, finishing *Yonnondio*, a novel she had begun as a 19-year-old girl. Theirs is a woman's story. But it is also a writer's story and encompasses many male writers.

The title story of Olsen's collection, *Tell Me A Riddle*, is one of the great pieces of American art. She also published a brilliant work of non-fiction entitled *Silences* which I passed on to Agnes Owens. The title refers to those precise gaps in a person's life, when you should be working at what you do, but simply cannot beg, steal or borrow the time.

She was a friend of Mary Gray Hughes, who in the mid 1970s sent me a rare edition of Olsen's *Tell Me A Riddle*. She did not tell me it was a rare edition. This collection of only four stories has had an impact on contemporary English-language literature, not only in the U.S.A. Her work offered a different way of seeing for myself, finding ways to hijack third-person narrative from the voice of imperial authority.

Prose fiction was exciting at this level. Somebody was punching fuck out ye but ye went away and attended the cuts, had a shower, and came back with Daddy's axe. Tillie's work was a weapon. The true function of grammar. Make yer point. Writers need to learn these lessons. If you do not then you will not tell the story. You might tell other stories but not the one you could be telling. These bastards think they own the language. They already own the courts. They own everything. They want to block your stories, and they will, if you let them. So go and do your work properly. Ye will need every weapon.

In my short-story collections, many stories began life as part of a longer narrative I hoped would become a novel. The problem becomes formal, particularly in 'I-voice' narratives. When there is no continuity in the writing the perspective of the central character shifts. It starts to feel like a different person. Even a slight variation can be too much. Eventually I gave up, transformed and finalised these sections. They became short stories in their own right.

Shifting the narrative voice back and forward, from first person to third, from third back to first, helped the process. This can resolve dramatic problems writers experience in 'I-voice' yarns. I wanted the central character active in a present adventure, not recounting the one about a mysterious stranger he once chanced to meet aboard a cargo ship to Borneo. I tried and rejected the present tense; locked into one dimension, behaviourist, static, lacking mystery, deterministic, non-existential. Just fucking philosophically naïve, like science fiction or world-weary detectives trudging the mean streets humming a piece of Mozart, to a backdrop of the theme from *Johnny Staccato*: the mental masturbation of the bourgeoisie, that was how I felt about the 'I-voice' present tense. Avoid it at all costs.

Go for richness, sophistication, infinite possibility: use the past tense properly, discover its subtlety. Learn yer fucking grammar! Do not be lazy! How does the verb operate in other language cultures?

There was a crucial factor that I liked about the shift from first to third party: you were left with a thought process; the central character had an inner life that seemed authentic. I just kept developing that third-party narrative, finding ways to embed the thought processes. This culminated in moves I made in *The Busconductor Hines*. There was something Joyce was doing, trying to be doing, Molly Bloom's soliloquy, *Finnegan's Wake*, it was just there how something, and it was just like eh, it was just fucking obvious man just how I could not quite say.

Alasdair Gray and I were having a pint together many years back and had a laugh about that. He knew exactly what I was talking about but could not quite get to what it was, that thing that we were talking about, maybe it was not a thing, maybe it was just a verb. It was certainly not the ineffable man that was a certainty, the ineffable is a fucking noun. That was 30 years ago, unless I have invented it all, probably I have.

The other novel from the early period was *A Chancer* which could only have been written prior to *The Busconductor Hines* otherwise it would have been very difficult, if not impossible. Yet I had to complete *The Busconductor Hines* before I could complete *A Chancer*.

Even to this day I get wistful about that other one, the unfinished third novel. I should have fucking finished it. I was just beat. If I had had the time, the space, if I could have found a way in. It needed all of that. The first, last or central section would have been the title story from my *Not Not While the Giro* collection.

There was even a fourth novel, about a private detective with a fondness for Russian literature. This guy is a black belt at every martial art, yet adored by women for his sensitive touch.

He is at home in every situation, able to cope with life on the street, degenerates of every profession, smiled at by prostitutes, respected by pimps and dealers, always at the ready to flummox university professors by quoting casually one of Pindar's lesser-known odes.

I wrote about 30 or 40 pages during that 1971–3 period.

When the bills pile up I trot it out and stride purposefully about the room. This one will be a movie! Hey Marie! Marie! Then I trip over the cat, try to kick him and fall on my chin. Where am I? Where is the computer? This damn novel will enter manifold translations. It will set us free forever!

Then I glance over the manuscript for ten minutes, yawn and make another cup of tea. Nothing against worldly private eyes, except how fucking boring they are. Imagine having to write such shite. It doesn't even warrant an exclamation mark. The ghostly appearance of one returned via Jeremiah Brown in *You Have to be Careful in the Land of the Free.*

Mary Gray Hughes was not so keen on my story 'Not Not While the Giro'. It was a bit too flashy, she thought. But I liked it. It was necessary, I had to work a way through the dimensions and that section was fundamental. If I had found the way through it, in it, and out it, then who knows. I should have explained to Mary Gray that originally it was a central section of an unfinished novel. But I always resisted explanations, as a rule of thumb. If you enter into one it usually means yer story has failed.